"You don't [...] goo[...]

Liz looked up in response to Max's statement.

"Spit it out, girl," Maria said. "My skin's green, my hair's about to turn green. I can take it."

"The human body replaces its surface layer of skin every fifteen to thirty days," Liz said.

"So we have to wait that long to get back to normal color?" Alex asked. "I suppose it could be worse."

Liz shook her head. "The alien cells seem to be bonding permanently with the new pigment-producing cells being produced, altering them in some fashion."

The silence in the room was powerful and heavy. Liz could feel the weight of the knowledge pounding down on her friends like a hammer.

"I might be wrong," she said softly. But she knew she wasn't.

"And if you're not," Max said, "how long until this change is permanent?"

"It's starting now."

ROSWELL™

Be sure to look for new titles in this suspense series

Don't miss any books in the original series:

ROSWELL HIGH

Available from POCKET BOOKS

ROSWELL™

LITTLE GREEN MEN

Dean Wesley Smith
and
Kristine Kathryn Rusch

From the television series
developed by Jason Katims

POCKET
BOOKS

LONDON • SYDNEY • NEW YORK • TOKYO • SINGAPORE • TORONTO

This book is a work of fiction. Any references to historical events, real people, or real locales are used fictitiously. Other names, characters, places, and incidents are the product of the author's imagination and any resemblance to actual events or locales or persons, living or dead, is entirely coincidental.

First POCKET BOOKS edition May 2002

POCKET BOOKS
An imprint of Simon & Schuster UK Ltd
Africa House
64–78 Kingsway
London WC2B 6AH

www.simonsays.co.uk

Printed in Great Britain by Bookmarque Ltd, Croydon

A CIP catalogue record for this book is available from the British Library

ISBN: 0-7434-5037X

In memory of D.C.
who was always strong, loving, and endearingly
grumpy . . .

LITTLE GREEN MEN

1

Dr. Donald Bridge snapped the latex glove off and tossed it into the garbage under the counter, then started toward the emergency-room desk as Denise, his nurse, put away the last of the equipment.

"You sure, Doc?" Mr. Archer asked, his voice still full of worry.

Bridge stopped and smiled at the older man sitting on the bed, the drapes that had given the area privacy now open. Archer's slight gut hung over his brown belt, making him look heavier than his measured weight. His undershirt was clean and white, accenting the hardened and leathery skin of a man who had spent many years in the sun. Bridge hoped he was in as good a shape at sixty-two as Archer was at this moment.

"Your heart is as healthy as they come," Bridge said confidently, as the older man slipped on his plaid shirt. "Trust me, the pains you have been feeling are just gas, and I've got something behind the desk that will do the trick."

The look of relief that slowly crept over Mr. Archer's face made Bridge smile. "Finish getting dressed and I'll meet you up front."

Archer nodded and slid off the bed. "Thanks, Doc."

Bridge turned and three steps later had entered the medical supply closet near the check-in area, where they kept all the sample-sized medications. Heartburn treatment was one of his favorites. Nothing dangerous, and very easy to cure in the short term. Too bad every patient who came through the front doors wasn't as easy to fix as Mr. Archer.

So far, Mr. Archer's bad case of heartburn was the worst problem Bridge had seen all day. It had only taken a few blood tests and fifteen minutes on the electrocardiograph to confirm that no heart incident was going on. If the day stayed this mild for just two more hours, Bridge knew he was going to make his plane. And then, all he had to do was enjoy six wonderful days of fishing in Alaska, far from the desert of New Mexico and the smell of emergency rooms and the late-night phone calls.

He could almost taste that wonderful fresh mountain air now.

"Doctor?" Anne said, her voice insistent.

Anne Haines was the emergency room's main receptionist, and over the last three years that Bridge had been here, he had never seen her ruffled over anything. She just kept people calm, did the paperwork flawlessly, and smiled more than she frowned. But now, she was using the tone she only used when she needed help at once in the front.

Bridge quickly stepped out of the supply closet and

into the reception area. During the three years he had been here since finishing his residency in Phoenix, he had seen every type of medical emergency come through those sliding glass doors. Gunshot wounds, stabbings, broken bones, concussions, and heart attacks. Facing the new and unknown problem was what kept him interested, and why he had picked emergency-room medicine in the first place.

But not in his wildest nightmare could he have imagined the sight that now greeted him. A man stood in front of the counter, with an upset woman beside him. And he was green.

Hands, face, ears, arms, all of his exposed skin was green. He looked like a miniature Jolly Green Giant from the old television ads.

Bridge didn't know whether to laugh or be worried.

Clearly the green man was more annoyed than in any sort of pain. And the annoyance was directed at his wife, more than likely the one who had insisted they come in. Both of them seemed to be in their early sixties and healthy, except for the man's color. There just wasn't anything healthy-looking about bright green skin.

He had on a short-sleeved shirt and slacks, she had on golf slacks and a light sweater over a pink blouse. They were dressed like they had just come from the golf course. Maybe something had happened there.

Bridge couldn't even remember reading about anything like this before. The man looked, at least across the counter dividing Anne's desk from the waiting area, as if all his skin pigment had changed colors. There was no immediate sign of a dye, and from the looks of these two, and how upset the woman seemed, this wasn't some sort of joke.

Bridge moved from behind the counter and into the front area, extending his hand toward the green man. "I'm Dr. Bridge," he said. "What happened?"

The green man shook Bridge's hand, his grasp firm and dry. "Greg Henry," he said. "This is my wife, Betty." He waved a green hand at the woman beside him. "Nothin' happened. I feel fine. Had a good round going, too."

"He just turned green, is all," Mrs. Henry said. "Head to foot. Right before my eyes."

"Well," Bridge said, making lists of possible causes in his head, "why don't you come on back, Mr. Henry, and we'll do some tests. Your wife can fill out the paperwork Anne needs, I'm sure."

"Thanks, Doctor," Mrs. Henry said, the worry in her eyes not far below the surface.

"Ahh, I feel fine," Mr. Henry said.

"Just do as the doctor suggests," the older woman said, her voice solid and forceful. "I don't want you glowin' in the dark and keeping me awake."

Mr. Henry waved a hand dismissing his wife's joke as both Anne and Bridge laughed.

Dr. Bridge escorted Greg Henry to a bed next to where Mr. Archer was just finishing putting on his shoes. Suddenly Anne's insistent voice again called out from the front desk.

"Doctor!"

A slight pause, then "Doctor!"

It was the most uncontrolled Bridge had ever heard her voice.

"Jump up here," he said to Henry, patting the emergency-room bed. "I'll be right back." He quickly headed back to the reception desk. There, both Anne and Mrs. Henry were staring at two more green people coming through the door.

And outside the glass entrance, a car pulled up and another green person got out.

The first thought that came to Bridge's mind was that his fishing trip was going to have to be postponed.

Then, as yet another car screeched to a halt outside, with another victim in the passenger seat, Bridge realized there was a lot more at stake here than his lost fishing trip.

With one hand on Anne's shoulder, he whispered in her ear. "Go to a back office and get General Drake at the base on the line. I think we have a real problem here. Then call in all the other doctors."

As she left to follow his orders, Bridge moved around the counter and did his best to calm the strangely colored people and their worried relatives, who were quickly filling the waiting area.

And as he did, Mrs. Henry slowly turned a pale shade of green.

Max knew something was going to go wrong today. He just knew it. The day had been too perfect so far, and for some reason, there hadn't been too many perfect days lately.

The sky was clear, the temperature just a little cool, his mom had been in a good mood. Perfect.

So what was going to go wrong?

He tried to shake the thought as he pulled open the front door to the Crashdown Café and stepped inside. He always felt comfortable here, as if he were walking into his own room at home. The smell of bacon that Michael was cooking on the fryer hung in the air like a thick perfume, flavoring just about everything.

Liz worked at cleaning the last few tables from the lunch rush, and Maria sat at the counter, piling her tips in neat stacks of dimes, nickels, quarters, and bills. Two tourists were in the front booth, just finishing their Saturn shakes while Alex read in the second booth, nursing a cherry Coke like it was the last drink he would ever see.

Everything normal.

Max let himself relax a little. He'd been having the bad feeling about the day since his family left for church this morning, but so far nothing was going wrong. He couldn't put his finger on what had sparked his unease, and now he was determined not to let it ruin a perfectly beautiful Sunday afternoon in early March.

Liz glanced over at him as the door closed and her eyes lit up, the smile filling her face, making her look even more beautiful to Max, if that was possible.

He loved the way she looked at him. He loved everything about her, actually. The long dark hair, her deep brown eyes, the smile that never seemed to be far away from her face when he was around. She lit up everything in his life, making every day more special than the one before. He couldn't imagine losing her. And yet that seemed to be what had happened this last year.

At times like this he wondered why they had so many

problems, why she kept pushing him away. Some day he hoped to understand that, if nothing else.

He waved without lifting his arm, smiling, as he headed for the booth with Alex.

"Cherry Coke?" Liz asked, brushing his arm as he went past. The touch made him grin even more. And wish for even more, even though he knew it couldn't happen.

"Thanks," he said, trying to hold on to her hand as she moved away, not really wanting to let it go.

Alex let out a sigh and shook his head. "You two are disgustingly cute at times, you know that?"

Max slid into the booth across from Alex, never taking his gaze off Liz. "At least we used to be," Max said.

Alex shook his head. "You know, I never have understood what happened."

"That makes two of us." Max settled back in the comfortable cushion of the booth and watched as Liz filled a glass with ice and some cherry syrup. After the events of the past few months, with the blue crystals in the cave and Christmas events in Phoenix, it was nice to just have everything calm.

He really needed to shake the foreboding feeling that something was going to happen.

There was nothing wrong with this day remaining calm enough that he and Liz might be able to spend some time together, to start to get things back on track. He couldn't remember the last time they had been able to do that.

Alex had gone back to his book. Max looked at it but couldn't see the title. Alex sure seemed absorbed in it, and he seemed calm, too. Nothing ever seemed to bother him.

"You superstitious, Alex?" Max asked.

"No," Alex said, not looking up. "But I don't walk under ladders if that's what you mean. It would be just my luck to have one fall on my head."

Max laughed. Alex wasn't as hapless as he made himself out to be.

"Why?" Alex frowned, marking his place with his left hand. "Is there something to be superstitious about?"

"No, I was just thinking it's too calm today," Max said. "And I'm afraid that means something is going to happen."

"Spring fever," Alex said, laughing lightly, "does that to all of us."

"Maybe you're right," Max said. He sure hoped so.

He took a deep breath and settled even more into the booth. He was probably just nervous because he hoped to patch things up with Liz tonight. He was going to invite her to spend some time with him, alone. Maybe then he could repair whatever had gone wrong.

Behind him the bell over the front door of the restaurant jingled, announcing a new arrival. Across the booth Alex glanced up, then went back to his book for a moment before yanking his head back up and staring over Max's shoulder.

Max didn't want to turn around. He knew that whoever had just come in threatened his night with Liz, threatened the peace he had hoped to get today, and if he ignored the person, he might just go away.

Then Alex broke into gales of laughter, and Max couldn't help himself. He swung around to look.

"What?" Kyle said, moving from the front door toward the counter.

Everyone in the restaurant was silent except for Alex

who was still laughing. All of them, including the two tourists, were staring at Kyle.

Max couldn't believe what he was seeing. Kyle's skin, at least his hands and face, were a pretty good shade of green. The kind of green you'd see on a ripe avocado.

"What?" Kyle demanded.

"Halloween is still a long ways off," Maria said, shaking her head and going back to counting her tips. "Take the body paint back, Kyle. It's not scary."

"Have all of you people gone mad?" Kyle asked.

"Maybe Kyle's in a play," Liz suggested, trying to placate him. Max hated it when she treated Kyle that way, as if he were important to her. Max still couldn't get the image of the two of them in Liz's bed out of his mind.

"I think you're too short to play Frankenstein," Alex said.

"Maybe he's the frog prince," Maria said.

Kyle looked puzzled. "Is this some kind of joke?"

"You tell us," Max said quietly.

"I'm not the one being funny here," Kyle snapped.

"Could've fooled me," Maria said.

"Will someone explain what's going on?" Kyle's voice rose in frustration.

"Your skin," Liz said, taking a tall cherry Coke past Kyle toward Max. "It sort of clashes with your blue shirt, if you know what I mean."

Kyle held up his hands and stared at them.

It was clear to Max that until that moment Kyle hadn't noticed his skin had turned green, which meant it must have happened fairly fast. Granted, Kyle wasn't the most observant person Max had ever met, but not noticing that

9

something had turned your own skin green was even beyond Kyle's abilities to ignore.

"Man, what did you get into?" Michael asked, coming out of the kitchen, wiping his hands on a towel before draping it over his shoulder. "You look like a bad St. Patrick's Day milkshake."

"I don't know," Kyle said, moving closer to Maria so he could look at his face in the mirror. It was also green, and seemingly getting darker by the moment.

"Pea soup does that to you," Maria said, glancing up at him before going on to finish her count. Then she started picking up the coins. "Never touch the stuff myself."

"Too much to drink last night, Kyle?" Alex asked. "You look a little *green.*"

Everyone but Kyle laughed.

"This isn't funny!" he said, not looking away from the mirror.

"Maybe not to you," Maria muttered.

Again everyone snickered.

For once, Max agreed with Kyle. Max wasn't at all sure this was funny.

Kyle pulled open his shirt and looked down at his own stomach. "I'm green all over!" He turned around so everyone could see his green chest and stomach.

"*All* over?" Michael asked, smiling and winking at Max and Alex and Liz.

"Don't go there," Maria said, her voice stern as she pointed her finger at Michael.

Michael laughed and moved down the counter, closer to Kyle.

Maria stood and, with a hand on Kyle's shoulder,

moved him around behind the counter to the sink. "Try washing it off."

"It could be worse," Alex said as Kyle ran his hands under the water. "At least you have a spring color."

Again everyone but Max and Kyle laughed, including the two tourists. But as Kyle lifted his wet hands up and it was clear nothing was washing off, Max knew this was very serious.

"I'd say we need to get you down to the hospital," Max said, scooting to the edge of the booth seat and getting ready to stand. "Let's find out what caused this."

"I agree," Liz said, also starting to frown at how the color hadn't washed off.

Kyle was staring in the mirror, looking stunned at the green face staring back.

"At least it's not turning your hair green," Alex said.

Maria just shook her head at the comment and Liz gave Alex a dark look.

"What?" Alex asked.

"You know," Max said, glancing at Alex across the booth, then doing a double-take. "You're not looking real healthy yourself right now."

"Nice try," Alex said, smiling.

Max wasn't kidding, but he didn't say that. Instead he reached across the table and tapped the skin on Alex's arm. It felt normal, but what should have been a pink color under the fingerprint had a faint green tinge to it.

"Feels green to me," Max said.

Michael again snorted. "Looks green from here."

Alex looked down at his arm. The smile drained from his face as he studied the backs of his hands. As everyone watched, the green seemed to grow darker on Alex's arms and face, becoming the prominent color of his skin, replacing the normal tones there just seconds before.

"Oh, man, I *am* turning green," Alex said, his voice low and shocked. "What's happening to me?"

In the booth behind Max the two tourists slid out, stood, and dashed for the door, banging it open as they rushed to get out of the restaurant.

"Come back any time," Maria said after them.

"Having customers turn green can't be good for business," Michael said.

This time no one laughed.

"It wasn't our fault," Liz said. "Kyle was green when he got here."

"No one mentioned it until I came in this door," Kyle said.

Everyone stared at one another—except Alex, who kept poking the skin on his arm.

"So what are we going to do?" Kyle asked. "I can't stay like this."

"We're going to take both of you to the hospital," Max said, standing and indicating that Alex should as well. "And I don't think we should waste any time."

"What happens if it has something to do with the cave?" Michael asked, staring at Max. "They were both in it, and that was only a couple of weeks ago. Are you sure going to the hospital is wise?"

Alex nodded, still holding his green arms away from his body as if letting them down might cause him to catch something. "Those blue crystals melted all over us."

Max didn't want to think about how close they had

come to losing both Kyle and Alex in that cave. But Michael did have a point. There could be a connection.

"Damn it!" Kyle said, "I knew I shouldn't have helped you. I knew it, I knew it! I've probably been infected with some alien life-form or something!"

"We don't know the blue crystals melting is what's causing this," Max said. "Do we, Michael?"

Michael shrugged and said nothing.

"Then what else could it be?" Kyle demanded, staring at Max as if Max had all the answers.

"Anything," Liz said, moving around the counter to comfort Kyle where he stood beside the sink. "This could be caused by anything. Something in the air, a government test, bad water, anything at all."

"That's right," Michael said. "For all we know, the entire town could be turning green."

"Yeah, right," Alex said, his tone disgusted. "A whole bunch of little green men in Roswell, New Mexico."

Again no one laughed.

"Actually," Liz said, "Michael just might be right." She pointed out the window.

Max followed where she was pointing. On the sidewalk across from the café a woman went past, heading for the nearby hospital at a very fast walk. She was a fairly bright shade of green under her blond hair. The sun made the color on her arms seem even brighter.

Max didn't know if he was glad to see it wasn't just Alex and Kyle, or not.

"Uh-oh," Alex said. "I'm sorry, Maria."

"About what?" Maria demanded.

Max turned back from the window and could see

exactly what Alex had meant. Maria was also changing, her light skin color growing darker and more green-tinted with each passing moment.

They all stared at her, the silence in the restaurant growing more and more intense.

"What?" Maria said, moving to brush a strand of hair off her forehead. As she did, she saw her hand. "No!"

The shout echoed a couple of times around the restaurant as Maria dived for the sink to try to wash the color away.

Liz moved to comfort her, but Maria brushed her off. "I've got to wash this off. This can't be happening to me. It can't! It just can't!"

"It doesn't wash off," Kyle said. "I tried, remember?"

"Let's head for the hospital," Max said. "Maybe they know what's happening. Michael, help Maria."

Michael moved to Maria's side and handed her a towel, then headed her away from the sink toward the front door.

"I can't be green," Maria said, staring at her arms and hands. "I just can't!"

"I'll still like you just as much," Michael said, shrugging.

She brushed him aside. "No, you don't understand, I hate green. I never wear green."

"Yes, you do," Liz said.

"Not this color green," Maria said. "This is shamrock green. I don't wear anything darker than lime green. It makes my hair seem washed out and dull."

"I think that's the least of your worries right now," Michael said.

Maria glared at him. "I am not supposed to be green.

Green is for characters in comic books, guys that fight Spider-Man. I can't be green."

Michael rolled his eyes, and Liz smiled nervously at Max.

"Let's go, people," Max said. He wanted to get out of here, to see how many other people in town were changing color—and if they were becoming any color other than green.

"It just can't be happening," Maria said.

"Don't worry," Michael said, heading her toward the front door, "we'll have you back to pale and sickly in no time at all."

"I need to stay and watch the restaurant," Liz said.

Max nodded. "We'll be back as soon as we can." He touched Liz's hand gently, then moved in behind Kyle.

With a gentle shove he pushed the stunned ex-football player toward the front door. Alex followed, then Michael and Maria.

The chime over the door jangled as they went out into the warm afternoon sun. It was a beautiful early March day, the leaves just starting to fill out on the trees.

Michael and Maria led the way, followed by Kyle and Alex. Max brought up the rear with one last look at Liz standing alone and stunned at the front window of the restaurant.

On the street people stared as they passed.

Two aliens escorting three green humans down the street. If it wasn't so serious, it just might have been funny.

2

A block from the hospital Max knew the situation was even worse than he had imagined. Cars jammed the tree-lined two-lane road that lead into the hospital parking lot. Some people had simply pulled their cars up onto the grass and left them there, deciding to walk the rest of the way.

Others sat in traffic, like commuters on a Los Angeles freeway, waiting, either the driver or one of the passengers green-skinned. With just under 50,000 people, Roswell wasn't tiny, but it definitely wasn't used to this kind of traffic near the hospital.

Kyle and Alex had the lead, with Michael and Maria and Max following as they passed stopped cars, speed-walking as if they were late for a class.

On the sidewalk ahead of them two green-skinned women were heading in the same direction, talking as if out for a walk in the park. Clearly whatever was causing people's skin to turn green was fairly widespread through the town. Now Max wished he had thought to turn on the television to see if it was a national problem, or even worldwide. Maybe some sort of strange solar radiation had caused this. There was just no telling.

No one seemed physically ill. Kyle, Alex, and Maria said they felt no different than usual. No headaches or stomachaches or exhaustion. If they hadn't been told that their skin had changed color, they wouldn't have even realized it.

So far, Max thought that was a hopeful sign. He was really worried that other symptoms would show up later—that the green skin was just some kind of weird warning sign of something more serious.

"This doesn't look promising." Alex said. The glut of cars was getting worse the closer the group got to the small hospital.

Three stories tall, white stucco, surrounded by a park-like setting and shade trees, Roswell Mercy Hospital was one of the nicer buildings in the town. And the most modern. Right now there were crowds of people milling around the emergency room entrance, both with green- and normal-colored skin. Two ambulances were stopped there, lights still strobing, back doors standing open.

"Yeah," Michael said, "maybe we should head back and just sit tight until they figure out what's going on."

"I'm not staying this color a second longer than I have to," Maria insisted. "Get me a doctor, stat."

Michael glanced at Max over Maria's head and just shrugged. Max could tell from Michael's expression that he thought Maria was overreacting, but Max didn't. She might be focusing on the color, but Max was worried his friends would suddenly develop other symptoms.

"We at least need to check inside, see what's going on," Max decided. He didn't add that he had no other ideas at the moment.

"Good," Maria said. "I really don't want to be the designated green person around here. People will start thinking *I'm* the alien."

Michael put his arm around Maria. "Fortunately, aliens aren't green."

"At least the ones we've met so far," she mumbled.

"Be careful, you guys," Alex said just before Max could.

Kyle had walked a few yards ahead of them. He stood, his hands on his hips, and stared at the people gathered outside the emergency room doors.

"We're not going in that way," he said. "The emergency room can make you wait hours on a slow day if you're not dying. And it doesn't look like any green person is dying."

"At least not yet," Alex said ominously.

"Not funny," Maria said, glaring at him.

"Didn't mean it to be," Alex said.

Max agreed with Kyle. He doubted they could get through the crowd at the emergency room door, let alone get a doctor to take a look at Maria and Kyle and Alex anytime in the near future. Two police cars were now trying to get to the hospital, their sirens working to nudge the stalled traffic out of their way. That was just going to complicate things here even more.

"Let's go around to the west side entrance," Max said, pointing off toward another parking lot on his right.

"Employee entrance," Michael said. "Good thinking."

Max just nodded, it might get them into the building, but he doubted from the looks of the mess around the emergency room door that any doctor would give them the time of day. But at the moment doing something was far better than doing nothing.

The Crashdown had never felt so isolated and empty and quiet. Outside the beautiful spring day signaled that life should be just fine, a day when people got out, enjoyed the sun, visited the attractions of Roswell, laughed, and played. Normally on a weekend afternoon like this one, there would be people coming in and out of the restaurant constantly, buying sodas, milkshakes, or just asking for a glass of water. They would be joking or having serious conversations, sweating or looking cool and relaxed. The place would feel alive.

But it didn't. Liz was there alone.

She should probably have been grateful that no one had come in since Alex, Kyle, Maria, Michael, and Max left. If someone did enter, she would have to handle the tables and the grill by herself. But she wouldn't mind the distraction right about now. Having no one to talk to was driving her crazy.

Liz could see a few people on the sidewalk, and some traffic, but nothing like normal at all. And no one seemed to be smiling or enjoying the sunny spring day.

She had tried to keep herself busy by wiping down the counter and every table, filling the salt shakers, and refilling the ketchup bottles. But now that every possible chore was done, there just wasn't much left except sit at the counter and worry.

She made herself a cherry cola, then sat on the end stool, trying not to look at the front door every few seconds.

The emergency room was going to take time. And if the next hour went by and no customers came in, she'd close up and join them there. For the moment she needed to pretend that life was going onward just fine, and this was nothing but a normal weekend.

But the silence and the empty chairs and booths made pretending hard.

Outside a man wearing a suit walked by, the skin on his face and neck bright green, almost matching his tie. He was headed in the direction of the hospital as well.

Nothing was normal.

She held her hand up and stared at her own skin. So far, whatever was causing this hadn't touched her. She didn't even know if it was a disease, or if it was contagious. Maybe she was going to turn green in an hour. There was no way of knowing.

It suddenly dawned on her that maybe this was happening to more than just Roswell. She moved around the counter and clicked on the radio. The news would tell her.

Music from the oldies station her mom kept the radio turned to filled the restaurant, giving it a false sense of life. She flicked the radio from station to station, pausing at each to listen for special reports.

Nothing but normal weekend programming all the way around the dial. It seemed that the problem had not yet reached that level of interest. But how could the local radio stations ignore people turning green? Maybe that meant the problem really wasn't as big as it had seemed at first. Maybe it was only happening in this part of town?

She left the radio tuned to the oldies station and went back to her stool. Even under normal conditions she hated slow times in the restaurant. She liked it more when the place was packed and she was busy every second. The time flew past then. Now it dragged by, each second seeming to tick slower and slower on the "Drink Coke" clock on the wall.

Behind her the chime over the door announced some-one had come in. She swung around, hoping to see the entire group. Instead Tess strode in, glancing around at the empty booths. Like the other alien teens, she was still her normal skin color. Whatever this was it didn't seem to be affecting any of them—yet.

"Wow," Tess said. "It's not often you see this place so quiet."

"Yeah," Liz said, turning back to sip her cola. "You want something?"

Over the last few months she and Tess had reached a sort of uneasy truce, but Liz still wasn't comfortable alone with Tess. Considering how close Max felt to Tess, Liz's unease bothered her. If Max trusted Tess, why didn't she?

"Nothing at the moment." Tess moved over and stood at the end of the counter next to Liz. "I passed two people headed over here who looked like they had turned green. What's going on?"

Liz quickly went through the events that had happened earlier. She ended with "Max told me to stay here and wait for them to return."

"Have you seen Isabel?" Tess asked.

"I think she went to a movie with some college guy," Liz said. "Max said they were coming in here after it was over."

Tess moved around and down beside Liz. "Doesn't Maria have her cell phone? You could call her and get an update."

"Good idea," Liz said, sliding off her stool and going around to get her own cell phone out of her purse behind the counter. She was amazed she hadn't thought of it a half hour ago.

It took her three tries before she finally gave up. All the circuits were jammed. Clearly this was a bigger emergency than the radio, with its benign oldies songs, was letting on.

She put the cell phone on the counter between her and Tess and slid back up on her stool.

"Now what?" Tess asked.

"We wait," Liz said.

"I hate waiting." Tess said.

"Tell me about it."

The hallways of the hospital were mostly empty, with a single nurse who seemed to be in charge of the entire section of rooms. There was no one with green skin in sight, and no crowds in this part of the building. Max didn't know if that was a good thing or a bad thing. The nurse, a solid-looking woman about Max's mother's age, was sitting behind a large counter. She glanced up at them without surprise, then pointed. "Emergency room down the hall. Keep turning to the left." Then she went back to work on the paper in front of her.

"Thanks," Max said.

The nurse nodded without looking up.

As they turned the corner of the hallway, the noise increased as if someone had turned up the volume of a speaker. A man was shouting over the rumble of others, while two calming voices tried to reassure the angry man.

"This doesn't sound good," Alex said.

Most of the doors along this area of the hallway had been closed, clearly to shelter the patients in their rooms from the noise.

Max had to agree that the sounds up ahead didn't sound positive. Anger in a hospital never seemed to bode well. It meant the situation was getting out of control, if it ever had been in control.

They rounded one more left corner and again the volume increased, as if they were suddenly in the middle of a large crowd at a basketball game. Down the hall Max could see the man who was shouting, facing off with a doctor and a nurse. Beyond them the waiting area of the emergency room was packed with green-skinned people, some holding the hands of spouses whose skin was still a normal color.

There had to be at least a hundred people jammed into that small space and the nearby halls, with more in the door and airlock. And none of them looked happy.

Max stopped, his friends following suit. The man waved a green arm in front of the doctor and shouted, "You're telling me you have no idea what's wrong with me? Why not?"

The doctor, clearly tired of arguing, turned to face the crowd. "Listen to me, everyone!"

But no one did. They all just kept talking, trying to be heard over the noise to the point where everyone was almost shouting.

"Listen up!" the doctor yelled, his voice powerful and carrying clearly.

For a moment Max didn't think anyone would stop, then slowly the noise died enough for the doctor to be heard.

"We're working as hard as we can to find out what is causing this skin-color change," the doctor said, his voice loud and forceful. "Right now, every doctor in the hospital is studying the problem, as well as the doctors at the base. We have some skin specialists flying in from Albuquerque. They're due on the base in an hour."

Max glanced at Michael, who only shook his head, clearly not happy with what he had just heard. It made sense to Max, though. Of course the military would be called in on a case like this. But he and Michael couldn't be caught inside a medical testing area. There was just too much of a chance of the doctors discovering the wrong things.

"I need everyone," the doctor said, raising his voice over the slightly increasing noise, "to just relax and work with us. As far as we know this is only a local problem, so there's an answer. You just have to give us time to find it and get you all back to your normal skin color."

"How long will that take?" someone shouted from near the emergency room door.

"We have no way of knowing," the doctor said, struggling to be heard over the growing noise. "If it's something simple, an hour or two, if not, it's going to take longer. That's all I can tell you."

That didn't please the crowd, but at least the man standing in front of the doctor had stopped yelling.

"I don't like the sound of this," Michael mumbled.

"Well, I'm not going anywhere," Maria said, "until they give me back my pasty white skin. I never thought I'd miss it."

"The skin seems to be the only thing affected," Max

pointed out. "No one looks really ill."

"So far," Alex said.

"I think the doctors would mention it. You know, put the really sick people in one area, the mildly sick in another, and the simply color-challenged in a third," Max said.

"Color-challenged?" Maria asked. "Is that an attempt at humor?"

"I think old Maxwell is trying for some political correctness," Michael said.

"Someone should probably tell him it's not working," Alex said.

"Why aren't you guys taking this seriously?" Max asked.

"What are we supposed to do?" Maria asked. "Go shout like that one guy has been?"

Kyle shook his head. "I, for one, don't feel like just sitting here and getting the runaround."

"And what exactly did you have in mind instead?" Alex asked.

"Sitting on my couch at home, in front of the television," Kyle said. "Someone call me when they find a cure and get this crowd taken care of."

With that he spun around and headed off down the hallway back in the direction they had come in. Max didn't blame him at all. In a way it sort of made sense, considering the mess they were facing down the hall.

"Are you going to let him just leave?" Maria asked, staring first at Michael, then Max.

Michael shrugged. "It's not my day to watch him."

"We can't do anything," Max said. "There's no point in forcing him to stay here if he doesn't want to."

"Uh, Max," Alex said, pointing to a nearby room, "you

need to look at this."

Max glanced in the direction Alex had pointed. Through the window of the empty room, Max could see the street running to the employee parking lot. Three open truckloads of army men went past. Every man seemed to be carrying a rifle.

"They're probably going to turn the hospital into a green-human's jail," Maria said.

"Quarantine," Alex agreed.

Max knew that what the army was about to do seemed very logical. If whatever was turning people green was a disease, then keeping it contained was the only answer. But he and Michael couldn't risk being imprisoned in the hospital, and being subject to medical tests.

"We've got to get out of here," Michael said. "And fast."

"We're going back the way we came," Max said. "Stick with me."

He turned and ran down the hallway toward where the nurse had given them directions. He had no doubt those soldiers would be unloading in the employee parking lot, on the opposite side of the building from the emergency room. That way, by the time anyone out front knew what was happening, it would be too late. They would be surrounded.

But that employee door was also the one they had come in.

Just before they reached the nurses' station, Max stopped and glanced down a side hall. It looked as if it led to some sort of closed café. And that meant there would be a kitchen entrance on the outside.

"This way," he said, keeping his voice low enough not

to let the nurse hear. Down the hall, he could see six men in uniforms with rifles starting through the employee entrance.

The group was running out of time.

The door into the café was locked. Michael pushed Alex aside and put his hand on the lock. Max glanced around while Michael quickly unlocked it.

They hurried inside. Max waited until last, making sure his green friends went in first.

The soldiers were getting closer, but they hadn't seen him yet. Finally he slipped through the door, shutting it quietly as the soldiers passed, their boots thumping on the smooth tile of the hallway.

"Lock that," Max said, pointing at the door. "And block it with a table."

"We're not planning on staying in here, are we?" Maria asked. She and Alex moved to push a table against the door as Michael relocked the door.

"No," Max said. "I'm just buying us a little time."

"Good," Maria said. "I hate cafeteria food."

Max led the way behind the counter and into the dark kitchen. It smelled of cleaning solution and old oil. Clearly this kitchen hadn't been used in some time. More than likely it was just a secondary place in case the hospital got full. No doubt they were going to open this up real soon, with all the people the military would probably be trapping in the hospital. Staying in here wasn't an option.

The back door had a dead bolt and a lock, both of which Max eased open as quietly as he could. No point in alerting a guard standing outside that they were coming.

He motioned that everyone behind him should stay

quiet, then eased open the door a crack.

The doorway was elevated slightly over the road so that trucks could back up to it and unload supplies easily. A staircase went down to the right toward a Dumpster. On the other side of the road Max could see some thick trees and brush. Beyond that he knew was the Country Club. From what he could remember from the one time he'd gone there with his father years before, it had a lot of trees and brush as cover as well.

So all they had to do was make it to the other side of the road and into the brush without being seen.

He eased open the door a little bit more and stuck his head out. To the right he could see one of the military transports, parked so that it blocked the road so no cars could leave. But there was no one in sight.

The left side was also clear to the end of the wing. The military was so concerned about rounding up everyone in the area of the emergency room that it hadn't yet set up guards at all the other entrances.

"We need to go fast and quick," Max said. "Follow me, and if we get split up, meet back at the Crashdown."

"And try not to let the military or any cop see your green skin," Michael said. "My guess is they're starting to round everyone up."

"If not yet, they will soon," Max agreed. "Let's go."

Making sure that both directions were still clear, he opened the door and in two steps was across the small loading platform, jumping down onto the road.

Alex was beside him, and Michael made sure Maria didn't stumble on the jump. So far no one had seen them.

Suddenly Max got the feeling they shouldn't do anything to draw any attention to themselves. "Walk naturally," Max said. "Stay together."

Moving casually as if they were out for a stroll, they walked across the road, down through a shallow drainage area that had been planed to look like desert, and then up into the more natural brush. Alex stuck his hands in his pockets. Maria did the same. She also put her head down, letting her hair cover her green face.

Michael and Max flanked Alex and Maria so that they wouldn't be as visible from the road. To Max's left he could see some soldiers facing the emergency room, guns at their sides, standing at parade rest. They were trying not to look threatening, but their intention was more than clear. No one was getting past them.

The soldiers didn't seem to notice the group as they ducked into some thicker brush.

Fifty paces later they reached the fence that surrounded the Country Club. Using his alien ability to manipulate matter, Michael cut them an opening large enough to crawl through.

Beyond the fence they found themselves in trees with a parklike setting. Just through the trees was the wide, lush green of a fairway.

"I think we made it," Michael said.

"Now we have to just make it back to the Crashdown without anyone seeing us," Maria said.

"It doesn't matter," Max said, "if regular people see us. Only police and military."

"He's right," Alex said. "This is happening so fast, I doubt the normal people on the street even know there's a problem. And from the looks of the number of people back there, not a large percentage of the city's population is affected."

"Yet," Maria said.

Max didn't like that thought, but he knew there was a good chance that many more people were going to turn green before this was solved. And if green was only the first step in some sort of disease, then this city, and maybe the entire country, was in trouble.

"Maybe we should go back in there," Alex said, staring at Maria and then turning toward Max. "We don't know if we're contagious or not."

"Staying in there, at this point, isn't going to help," Max said. "We'll keep you two isolated at the Crashdown, just in case."

"Besides," Michael said, "the food's better at the restaurant."

Alex nodded, clearly not certain, but not wanting to go back into that mess any more than Max did.

"You bragging about your greasy fries again?" Maria asked as she and Michael headed through the trees toward the fairway.

"You don't have to go far to get better than hospital food," Alex said, glad to think about something else.

Before Michael could say anything, Maria patted his arm and smiled at him. "I think your cooking is better than hospital food. Don't you, Max?"

"No comment," Max said, smiling as Alex and Maria laughed at the frown on Michael's face.

"You guys are finding this funny now," Michael said, "but if the army stays, we're in big trouble."

"I know," Max said, the smile leaving his face. "Believe me, I know."

3

After ten minutes of sitting beside Tess and saying nothing, Liz decided that the situation was going to drive her crazy, so she moved around behind the counter and started cleaning the ice-cream machine. It was a job usually reserved for later in the evening, but there didn't seem to be much point in waiting now. No one but Tess had entered the Crashdown in over an hour.

Tess sat at the counter, sipping on a glass of water and not saying anything at all. Her attention shifted from watching Liz to staring at passing cars outside. There wasn't much the two of them had to talk about on good days. And so far today had not turned out to be a good day.

The radio station still said nothing about people turning green. Liz wasn't sure if that was a good sign or a bad sign.

The jingling of the bell over the door almost made Liz drop the blender blade back into the ice-cream machine. She eased it into the sink and turned around to see Sheriff Valenti come in.

He was wearing his usual jeans and denim shirt, his hat pulled low over his face. It took Liz a moment to be sure that his skin hadn't yet turned green.

"Have either of you seen Kyle?" he asked.

Tess glanced at Liz, who wiped her hands on a towel as she nodded. "He went with Alex, Michael, Maria, and Max to the hospital about an hour ago."

Liz could tell the news was not what Valenti wanted to hear. Not at all.

"Which one of them had—" He hesitated, then said, "—a problem?"

"Kyle, Alex, and Maria all had their skin turn green," Liz said.

Valenti sighed, then shook his head. "I was afraid of that."

"Do you know what's causing this?" Tess asked.

"No," he said, moving over and standing at the end of the counter, his voice lowering as if he was telling them information he didn't want anyone else to hear, even though there was no one else in the restaurant. "But the military is quarantining off the hospital. If they're in there, they're not getting out until this is solved."

"Oh, no," Liz said. The thought of Max and Michael trapped inside a medical quarantine wasn't good. That was far, far too risky a place for them to be. Valenti knew the stakes involved. At first he had pursued the alien teens but eventually he had understood they meant no harm and had become friend and protector.

"The doctors are saying this is nothing but a shift in skin pigmentation they can't explain," Valenti said, "and is not dangerous in any way."

"But?" Tess asked.

Valenti frowned. "But the military is insisting on treating it like a contagious plague."

"Typical government thinking," Tess said, the disgust clear in her voice. "When did it become government policy to round someone up because of the color of their skin?"

Liz and Valenti both looked at her in surprise. That comment made her seem truly alien, even though she was raised in the United States, just like the other two were.

Liz didn't want to remind her of the history of her country and all the times that the government had rounded people up because of their skin color. Better to just let Tess vent her anger.

"Do they know something we don't?" Liz asked Valenti.

"Who?"

"The government. Does this get worse? Is the skin the only thing affected?"

He shrugged. "I've been trying to find that out, but I'm no longer in charge here. They don't have to tell me anything. But they seem as baffled by this as I am, and from some of the comments I've overheard, it seems that Roswell is the only place affected."

At that moment the door opened, again sending the bell jingling. Maria, her skin a bright green, came through first, followed by Alex, then Michael, then Max. Clearly they were being careful, with Max checking the street, and Alex and Maria instantly heading for the counter. They ducked behind it, as far from the window as they could get.

Liz couldn't believe the relief she was feeling, even though Maria and Alex were still green-skinned.

"How did you get out?" Tess asked.

"Where's Kyle?" Valenti asked at the same time.

Michael answered. "We snuck out through the kitchen right as they were sealing off the hospital."

"We had to duck a few military transports on the way back here as well," Max said. "But I don't think anyone saw us. Kyle left and went home."

Valenti nodded. He looked relieved. "Good. My suggestion is you guys stay out of sight here."

"And do what?" Maria said. "I look like a lime Popsicle."

"I'll keep you informed as to what is going on," Valenti said. "But first I'm going to go check to make sure Kyle made it home and give him the same advice."

"Thanks, Sheriff," Max said as Valenti turned and headed for the door.

"Just don't do anything stupid," Valenti said. "Stay low and inside."

"As if I'm going out in public looking like a green apple," Maria said.

"Popsicle," Alex said.

"Whatever."

Isabel liked watching the movie's credits all the way to the end. It was a habit that no one else bothered with, and often she ended up alone in the theater when the lights came up.

This time Rob had stayed with her, at first standing in the dark and putting on his coat, then sitting back down and waiting, pretending to be as interested as she was in the endless list of names scrolling by. It was a first date for them, so what choice did he have?

Rob was a freshman at New Mexico State in Albuquerque who had graduated last year from her high school. She had seen him around, but until he came back on spring break, it had never occurred to her to go out with him. Something about that half year he'd spent in college made him much more attractive. He had filled out and was no longer the rail-thin kid with big glasses. Now he wore contacts and dressed well and had a smile that could light up a room and make her heart flutter.

So far, with a quick lunch before the movie, he had been great company. Funny and not pushy at all.

As the copyright notices rolled past and the theater lights came up, he said, "Fun movie."

Isabel stood and turned to face him. She was about to say that she agreed, it had been fun, when his appearance brought her up cold.

His face was a bright shade of green, as was his neck, his arms, and his hands. He clearly hadn't noticed.

Then she felt an odd suspicion. Had he done this as a joke? He could have put on face paint in the men's room when he disappeared in the middle of the movie. But if he had, why would he? It didn't make sense.

"What happened to you?" she blurted.

He frowned, his green skin wrinkling just like regular skin. It didn't look like he was wearing pancake make up. "What do you mean, what—"

At that moment he glanced at his hand, and the shock seemed to almost knock him back into the seat.

"Is this some sort of joke?" he demanded, his voice clearly barely containing the anger and panic as he stared at both arms, then pulled his sleeve up to see the green skin there as well.

Since that had been her initial response, and since he

seemed surprised by the change, Isabel felt a funny kind of relief. Relief that he wasn't playing a game.

"I don't think so." Isabel held up her arm up to make sure it was still her normal color. Then she said, "Your face is green as well."

His hands went instantly to his face, as if touching it would tell him the color he couldn't see. Then he unbuttoned two buttons on his shirt and opened it. The skin on his chest was green. He tried to rebutton his shirt, but his hands were shaking too much.

"Come on," she said, "let's get you outside where the light's better."

"So your friends can laugh at their joke?" he demanded. "I don't think so."

"This isn't a joke anyone I know would do," Isabel said, staring into his angry eyes, standing her ground with him. She could see just how mad he was, and she didn't blame him. Not in the slightest.

"Then what is this?" He held up his green hands in front of her face.

"I don't know," she said, trying to keep her voice calm in the empty theater. "You may be having a reaction to something from lunch. Let's get you checked out."

He stared at her for a moment, the anger slowly draining away. "No joke?"

"No joke," she said. "Are you feeling all right?"

"What do you mean, all right?" he asked. "I've just turned green."

"I mean, are there other symptoms?"

He paused, took a few tentative breaths, then shook his head. "I feel normal."

"Well, there's that at least," she said. "Come on. Let's take you to the emergency room."

"What can they do?" he asked.

"I don't know," she said. "Maybe they know about some special popcorn butter that turns people green. Or something. I just think you should get this checked out."

He nodded, the look on his oddly unfamiliar green face telling Isabel that the seriousness of the situation was suddenly sinking in.

She took his arm and turned him toward the entrance. He seemed to stumble for a moment, then caught his stride as the two of them walked side-by-side out into the lobby of the six-plex.

The place was empty, which bothered Isabel more than it would have under normal circumstances. There wasn't anyone behind the candy counter, no kids at the half dozen video games. The front door stood open, a light breeze blowing in.

Outside there were only a few cars left in the parking lot, one of them Rob's new Volkswagen Beetle. People should have started arriving by now for the next shows. But that clearly wasn't happening.

"You better get to the hospital," a voice said from behind them.

They both spun around to see a woman who had taken their tickets standing to one side of the candy counter, half-hidden by a wall, as if afraid to come out.

"Why?" Isabel demanded.

"That's where the other green people went," the woman said. "Go to the hospital."

"There were others who turned green?" Rob asked.

"Yeah, three or four in your show alone," the hidden woman said.

Whatever had happened to Rob was happening to others as well. She glanced at Rob. For the first time fear filled his eyes.

"Come on," Isabel said, nudging him toward the door. "It's only a few blocks away. We might as well leave your car here and walk." The last thing she wanted was him trying to drive a car with his mind lost in another problem.

He nodded. "Good idea." His voice sounded like a controlled whisper, but she could tell he was quickly coming back to his senses. "Can't walk around like a giant pickle the rest of my life."

She forced a laugh at his lame joke. "Make up does wonders."

He looked at her, the fear still in his eyes, but the courage coming back clearly, covering the fear, pushing it down. He blinked at her, then smiled, his white teeth a stark contrast to his green lips. "Yeah, green face and blue eye liner. A new trend."

This time her laugh was a little stronger.

By the time they walked the two blocks to the hospital, they were both laughing and being very silly.

At the entrance to the hospital drive it became clear that a large number of people were affected by what was happening. Cars blocked the road and were parked up on the grass. Three army men stood near the entrance, while other police and soldiers held posts along the hospital grounds, Isabel noticed. All of them carried weapons.

"Oh, no," Isabel said.

"What's the army doing here?" Rob asked.

"Look," Isabel said. "Maybe this wasn't such a good idea after all."

"If the army's here," he said, "doesn't that make this like that movie *Outbreak* or something? Does that mean this is deadly?"

Isabel shook her head and started to back away. "I can't stay here."

Rob grabbed her arm. "Isabel. I can't do this alone. Besides, you were next to me the whole time. You might have caught this thing."

"I don't get sick," she said reflexively.

"Neither do I," he snapped.

Their argument was calling attention to them. One of the soldiers came over. Isabel tried to shake out of Rob's grasp, but he held on tight and she didn't want to make a scene.

"Follow the driveway to the main entrance," the soldier said.

"And what will happen there?" Isabel asked.

"Just follow the driveway," the man said, his voice showing no sign of compassion. He had just given them an order with no other choice.

Rob pulled her slightly into motion, heading down the sidewalk toward the hospital. "Looks like I'm far from the only one having this problem. Somehow that makes me feel better."

Isabel only nodded. It didn't make her feel better at all. She had dealt with the government before. Having the army involved in this meant only trouble as far as she was concerned. In fact, it scared her. This wasn't the place for her to be, but there was no way she could tell Rob that now.

They were herded like cattle down a path lined by armed soldiers until they reached the front door. Inside a man with a rifle stood beside a nurse who looked stressed. There were at least ten other soldiers in the lobby area. Clearly the army was afraid of green people. The question was why.

The nurse asked both of their names, wrote Rob's name on one sheet, Isabel's on another. There were many names above theirs on both sheets.

"You go down the hall to the left and into the central court," she said to Isabel. Then she looked at Rob. "This gentleman will take you to the ward on the left."

The soldier standing next to the nurse nodded and pointed for Rob to follow him.

"Not until I get some answers," Rob said. "What has happened to my skin?"

"That's what we are trying to find out," the nurse said. "And we'll be able to do that faster if you help us."

Isabel knew a repeated speech when she heard one. Clearly this had been happening for hours, more than likely the entire time they had been in the movie.

Rob snorted but said nothing.

"Is there a reason we can't stay together?" Isabel asked.

"Until we get some answers," the nurse said, "the doctors think it is better to keep affected people separate from those who show no visible changes."

"Quarantine," Rob said.

"Yes, in a way," the nurse said, nodding. "Now, please, go with the soldier."

Behind them the door opened and two more people with bright green skin entered. Isabel could tell they were clearly a couple, both in their midforties, both looking very worried and frightened.

Rob glanced at the couple, then turned back to the nurse. "Is there a way for me to call my parents?"

"Phones are available in the ward," the nurse said. "You're welcome to call your family."

He nodded and looked at Isabel, clearly not knowing what to say. She could tell he did not want to be alone with this.

"Are there a lot of people here?" she asked the nurse.

"Yes," the nurse said.

Isabel looked at Rob, then back to the nurse. "Are you sure I can't go with him?"

"Yes, I'm sure," the nurse said. "Believe me, honey. You don't want to go there. Green's not your color."

Green was her color. She wore it a lot. And she was fairly sure she'd be okay. But she said nothing.

"It's okay, Isabel," Rob said, sounding stronger than he had. Maybe he felt better knowing that he wasn't the only one.

"I'll see you when this is over," Isabel said.

"Good," he said. "I'm sorry about this."

"Why?" she asked.

"It's not how I wanted our first date to end."

"Me, either," she said softly.

They stared at each other for a moment. His eyes looked familiar at least, dark and brown and tender. Then he turned, following the soldier down the hall.

Isabel watched for a moment. It seemed like Rob's skin had become even greener. He was walking with confidence, but she didn't know how much of that was bravado.

How terrifying this must have been for him.

How terrifying it was for her. This was the worst place she could be.

But the best thing she could do at the moment was follow instructions. She headed toward the open courtyard the nurse had indicated. It was a square surrounded completely by building. It had grass and trees and rocks and a lot of flower beds, some just starting to show spring growth. It also had soldiers stationed at the doors around the large square, clearly there to make sure no one got out.

The soldiers stationed at the door she went through didn't even acknowledge her, not that she expected them to.

From what Isabel could tell there were about a hundred people in the large courtyard, most sitting together in small groups, talking. A few were stretched out in the sun, sleeping. Coffee and soft drinks had been put on a table near one door on the other side. She could hear a few birds chirping and people speaking softly, as if a meeting was about to begin.

Isabel walked toward the center, looking around. There wasn't anyone she recognized enough to talk with, and no one made eye contact with her for very long, so she moved into the shade of a tree. There she pulled out her cell phone and dialed the number of the Crashdown. More than likely whoever was there could pass the word to her family about what had happened to her. She doubted she was going to be getting out of here any time soon. Max and Michael were going to be worried, but she was sure she could convince them to do nothing at the moment. She wasn't in any danger of being tested for anything yet.

The circuits were busy.

She tried again.

No luck.

She tried her home number, then Maria's cell-phone number.

The annoying busy signal, followed by the helpful digitized female voice, informing her that all circuits were busy now and that she needed to try her call later, came on again.

Whatever was happening was large enough to jam the phone lines. Or maybe the military had jammed them. No way for her to know.

All she knew was that she hated being out of touch. No one knew where she was. But she wouldn't panic. If there were a lot of green people, it would be some time before the government started testing the ones who hadn't changed color.

She sat down on the grass, her back against the trunk of the tree, and watched as two more people came in. People with perfectly normal skin, clearly here with someone whose skin had turned green.

So why were only some people having this problem? Or was it going to affect them all, eventually? Somehow there was a link, a logical connection, but finding it was going to be very hard, and was going to take time. That much she was sure of.

About fifty paces away a woman said, "Oh, no!" very loudly.

The woman stood, her arms away from her body as if she had been dipped in something she didn't want to get on her clothes. Her skin was starting to turn green. Those around her stepped back slightly as she stared at her arms.

"I think you'd better get back into the hospital," one woman near her said, moving to help her.

The greenish-tinted woman nodded, clearly in shock at what was happening to her.

Isabel and the rest of the people trapped in this court-yard watched the two women as they headed toward the door, where a guard motioned for the green-skinned one to follow him, leaving the other behind.

Silence filled the courtyard for a moment, then people went back to talking in hushed tones.

Isabel again tried the Crashdown number.

All circuits were busy.

Even with the hundred people around her, she hadn't felt this alone in a long, long time.

Max really had no idea what to do next.

Liz had told them her parents were out of town for the weekend, so upstairs would be as good a place as any for them to hide Maria and Alex. They had gone up there while he stayed downstairs and talked to Michael for a minute. Michael had no ideas either.

"We're playing this one by ear," Michael had said. "And we're not involved at the moment, so let's try to keep it that way. Okay, Maxwell?"

Max had agreed. The further they stayed out of this entire mess, the better off they would be. But that still didn't answer any questions. Why hadn't Liz turned green? Why didn't this affect him and Michael and Tess? Were they just lucky? Or was their alien physiology going to make them the only white-skinned people left in the city in a few?

And where was Isabel? She hadn't checked in with anyone,

and that wasn't like her. She had gone on a date with some college kid earlier. Max just hoped she hadn't been affected and wasn't now trapped in the hospital by the army.

The army would be testing people. If Isabel got trapped in the quarantine, she'd be in big trouble.

Questions and no answers. He hated that.

With Michael staying downstairs to guard the restaurant in case anyone came in, Max went upstairs to join the others. He found them all in Liz's bedroom.

Maria was sitting at Liz's dressing table, staring at herself in the mirror. Liz and Alex were sitting on the bed; Tess was standing near the window.

"Halloween costume, for sure," Maria said, touching her green cheek and then letting go. "All I'll need is black lipstick and a fake nose. Then, if I can find a dark cape and pointed hat, I'll make the perfect witch."

"Broom," Alex said. "You forgot the broom."

"If I'm still like this by next fall, I'm going to need a lot more than a broom," Maria said. She looked over at Max standing in the doorway. "So why don't you cure us?"

He'd already thought of that possibility. And he didn't much like the idea, after what had happened in Phoenix. It was draining, and gave him insights into anyone he healed. He didn't really want that much information about either Maria or Alex. And besides, he had his doubts as to the success of even trying.

He glanced at Tess, who only shrugged. She clearly had no better idea either.

Liz smiled at him. "No matter how much I like green, I think it might be the best idea."

"You like green?" Alex asked, smiling at her, his white

teeth a sharp contrast to his green lips. "Maybe I should stay like this, then?"

"You can do what you please, but I want my old skin back," Maria said. She looked at Max. "Please? At least give it a shot."

He nodded. "I'll try, unless someone can come up with a reason why I shouldn't."

No one said a word.

Liz smiled at him, clearly a little worried. It wasn't dangerous, but she knew how much healing someone drained him. It had taken him a long time to recover after the Phoenix hospital visit.

He moved over and put his hand on Maria, just under her chin, his palm flat against her upper chest. She leaned back and closed her eyes, bracing herself on the dressing table.

"No tickling," she said.

"Here goes," he said.

No one said anything.

Liz smiled at him, nodding.

He closed his eyes and focused inward, letting his mind dig up the healing energy he knew lay inside of himself. Every time he did this it felt like a heat rush, as if the energy was digging down inside his soul and pulling up strength.

He sent the energy through his hand and into Maria, letting the light and feeling of it blend into the two of them, pulling them together.

Closer and closer.

Flashes of her life snapped through his mind.

Her mother through her eyes, smiling down at her

when she was a child.

Michael, the first time she saw him.

Liz as a junior high school girl.

The restaurant.

School.

All quick images, quick emotions, quick feelings, giving him much more information about Maria than he wanted.

Then he was done.

The light and energy seemed to suddenly be gone, and he stepped back, catching himself before it turned into a stagger. The strength he had felt a moment before now left him almost too weak to stand.

Maria glanced at her arms, then up at Max. "It didn't work!"

"I was afraid of that," Max said, his voice soft.

"Why didn't it work?" Liz asked, moving to stand beside him, bracing him as his energy slowly returned.

"Because she's not sick," Tess said. "Of course."

That was what Max had been afraid of. He let himself lean against Liz as his strength slowly came back. They had been thinking of this problem as a disease, simply because the skin changed. But no one had actually complained about any aches or pains.

"What do you mean, I'm not sick?" Maria's voice rose. "I'm green. You don't get much sicker than that."

"Your skin was pale before," Tess said, staring at her.

"So?" Maria asked, glancing first at Tess, then at Max.

He didn't have the energy to give her an answer at the moment.

"Paler than mine," Alex said, sighing. "I understand.

Green skin doesn't mean you are sicker now than when your skin was pure white with freckles. Or any sicker than a black person, or any one with any skin color."

"I'm green!" Maria shouted. "I wasn't green and now I am. That has to mean something's wrong, doesn't it?"

"Doesn't mean you're sick, however," Alex said.

"Come on, Alex," Maria said, turning to him. "Aren't you freaked out by this?"

"By you being green?"

"You know what I mean!" She held out her arms. "*Look* at me. Look at *us*. This is clearly an illness."

"If you had been sick," Max said, "I would have been able to cure it."

"It would seem," Tess said, "that green just may now be your natural color."

"That's not funny!" Maria said.

"It wasn't supposed to be," Tess said.

4

"Ouch," Alex said, shaking his arm.

"Oh, you big baby," Liz said, laughing. She had just taken a very thin skin sample from him and was going to try to compare his skin with a sample of her skin under a microscope. She figured at this point, there was no use in just sitting around. No one was coming in the restaurant, Maria was still sitting at the dressing table, staring at her green face, and Max and Tess had gone downstairs to talk with Michael and see if they could get in contact with Isabel.

She had felt she needed to do something.

She had no doubt that she would find anything different than anyone else, but she at least wanted to see what was happening with Alex and Maria's skin. She had studied skin color in science class a year ago, and she had found it fascinating. She had had no idea then that her old textbook and interest in skin color would come in handy this way.

"Well, it hurt," Alex said. "Just because it's green doesn't mean it doesn't have nerve endings."

"I never would have guessed," she said, patting his knee before adjusting the slide. "I took the same amount off of my arm, so we're even."

"Women deal with pain better," Alex said.

"We don't whine about it as much, that's for sure," Maria said. "Liz, what kind of makeup do you have?"

"Nothing that will cover your green," Liz said, not looking up from her work. She didn't want to be distracted right now.

"My base is really light," Maria said. "Yours would be darker. It might work."

"I don't wear base," Liz said.

"Hmmm." Maria leaned toward the mirror.

"Maybe you should try some of that white stuff," Alex said. "You know, like Kabuki actors."

"Kabuki actors?" Maria asked.

"Or Goth chicks," Liz said. She finished creating the slide. She had to be careful because the two samples were both small and very thin. And she had put them very close together on the slide.

"You have some of that?" Maria asked.

"No-o," Liz said, making the word into two syllables. "Now leave me alone. I'm working here."

"Yeah," Maria said. "Like you can find stuff the experts can't."

"Come on, Maria," Alex said. "Liz has information the experts don't have."

"Like the fact that there are aliens in Roswell?"

"Yeah," Alex said.

"Are we blaming this on aliens, too, then?" Maria said. "Do you think a friend of the Skins poisoned the water supply?"

"Anything's possible," Alex said quietly. "After all, it is the skin that's changing."

Liz felt a shudder run through her. "Remember when I asked for that silence thing?"

"You just asked us to leave you alone," Maria said. "Mind if I dig through your makeup drawer?"

Liz did mind, but she didn't say anything. Right now, she wanted to concentrate, and if her makeup kept Maria quiet, then that would help.

Carefully she put the slide on her microscope. Max used to tease her about that microscope, saying it wasn't normal equipment for most high school kids. But then, she wasn't most high school kids.

From what she remembered from class, the pigment-producing cells on humans were on the surface layers of skin. These cells were stuck between the normal skin cells in what she remembered being the basil layer of the epidermis. In other words, not very deep, thank heavens for Alex.

He would have really complained if she had to take off all seven layers.

The skin cells that created color were called melanocytes. They synthesized a pigment called melanin that reflected light. Something had changed the property of those cells in Alex's skin, causing the pigments to reflect light in such a fashion that made his skin look green.

Carefully she moved the slide into position and adjusted the focus. Nothing at all looked abnormal with any cells in Alex's skin. The two samples were basically the same, except his showed green melanin in the cells and hers normal-colored melanin. This was going to be a lot harder for the scientists to solve than she had first imagined.

"Well?" Alex asked.

"I don't see anything obvious," she said. "And this microscope isn't powerful enough to really get down inside the cellular level."

"But it's normal?"

"There's nothing normal about this color," Maria said.

"It's normal," Liz said, reassuring him as much as she could under the circumstances. "Except the melanin pigments in your cells are somehow reflecting light in such a way as to make it look green."

"What would cause a skin cell to change like that?"

"Yeah, good question," Maria said.

"I have no idea," Liz said, glancing up at Alex, then over at Maria. "It might not be the cell. It might only be the melanin. Green is a combination of blue and yellow light bands. Yellow and different shades of brown are normal melanin reflected colors, but blue isn't. And neither is green."

"Okay," Alex said, holding up his hand for her to stop. "You lost me a few colors back. What exactly is this melanin stuff?"

"Oh, oh, science class," Maria said.

Liz laughed and explained. "Melanin is the pigment put out by your skin's melanocyte cells."

"Melanocyte cells?" Alex asked.

"They are like little pigment factories," Liz said, "scattered throughout the rest of your skin cells."

"Got it," Alex said.

"Even I got that," Maria said.

Liz went on. "The pigment is bound to a protein after it is produced to form what are called melanosomes. Those are spread out over your skin layer to give it color. Mostly this entire system is designed to protect the human body from ultraviolet rays."

"Wow, now you lost me," Alex said. "What makes one person's skin real pale like Maria's, and another person dark? Is it the number of these mela-things?"

"Actually, no," Liz said. "All of us, no matter what our skin tone, have about the same amount of pigment-producing melanocyte cells."

"You're kidding," Maria said. "You're sure I'm not short on them, since my skin is usually so pale."

"Nope," Liz said. "What makes the difference is genetic programming in the cells. At birth, our bodies are set to produce a certain amount of pigment. How much of that pigment is spread around over your skin is also already determined. The more pigment, the darker the color, the greater the protection from ultraviolet."

"So what causes a suntan?" Alex asked.

"From what I remember," Liz said, proud of the fact that this information had sunk in from last year, "when too much ultraviolet radiation hits the melanin, it oxidizes and darkens. And at the same time causes the melanocyte cells to produce more melanin, and thicken the skin. It's a natural skin-protection system. The darker the skin, the more resistance to burns."

"So I sunburn easy because I have very little of this pigment stuff in my skin?" Maria asked.

"Yes," Liz said.

"Geez," Maria said. "Someone should find a way to

bottle this stuff. It would be better than suntan lotion."

"Maybe they have," Alex said.

Liz looked up, feeling appalled. "You think someone did this on purpose?"

"I don't know what to think," he said.

"I'm sure I'd find sign of it," Liz said, but she wasn't. Not really.

"So, what might cause a color change like this?" Alex asked, holding out his arm and looking at the green skin.

"I honestly have no idea," Liz said. "There's some change to how the light is reflected by the melanin, that's for sure. If I remember right, the pituitary glands put out hormones that cause pigment formation in the melanocyte cells. It might be something there."

"Pituitary glands?" Alex asked, looking discouraged. "This is going to be difficult, isn't it?"

"I'm afraid so," Liz said. "I have no idea what's causing the change, and there are real scientists, with better equipment, working on this right now, I'm sure."

"I hope so," Alex said.

"Me too," Maria said, "no offense."

"So do I," Liz said, going back to studying the cells under her microscope, looking for anything that might give her a clue. But nothing was there. The two samples, except for color, looked strikingly the same.

Then suddenly, blue cells appeared on the side where before there had been none. Each blue cell surrounded a pigment-producing melanocyte cell.

She couldn't believe what she was seeing. Cells couldn't just appear in a skin sample like that. It wasn't possible.

"Any luck?" Max asked, appearing in the doorway.

"I know more about skin coloring than I ever wanted to know," Maria said.

Liz looked up at Max, trying to make herself focus. The only thing that had changed was him coming into the room. Somehow, his presence had coincided with cells that had been invisible before appearing. But that didn't seem possible.

"If she asks for a skin sample," Alex said, "don't let her take it. She's a menace!"

"Oh, poor baby," Maria said.

Liz ignored their banter, trying to get her mind to focus on what she had just seen. She looked back into the microscope. The blue cells were still there. She had to find out if her barely formed theory was right.

She looked at Max. "Go back to the top of the stairs and stand there until I call you back."

Max frowned, confused. "What?"

"Just do it." Liz said, She didn't want to explain anything until she made sure. "I want to test something."

Max glanced at Alex and shrugged, then turned and left.

"You've gone nuts, haven't you?" Maria asked.

"Maybe, but I have a hunch," Liz said.

After a moment Max shouted, "I'm at the stairs."

She looked back through the microscope at her two samples. The blue cells covering the pigment-producing cells in Alex's green skin were gone, as if they had never been there. Or more than likely, they were still there, but she just couldn't see them with the equipment she was using.

Keeping her eyes on the slide, she shouted, "All right, come back in!"

"I hope you're not just having fun with me," he said, entering the room again.

As he did the blue cells covering Alex's pigment-producing cells in the skin sample reappeared. Somehow, Max's presence made them visible.

She looked up at Max, the shock of what she was thinking making her short of breath.

"What?" Max asked.

"Yeah, what?" Alex asked. "Something change?"

"Max is back in the room," Maria said. "That's a change."

"This skin thing is alien related," Liz said, blurting out the thought that had been forming in her mind.

"No way," Max said. "Why would you think that?"

"Take a look," Liz said, moving carefully not to bump the microscope and its settings as she moved aside. "Alex's skin sample is on the left, mine is on the right."

Max leaned in and studied the image of the two skin samples through the microscope. "There's a blue cell over some of the cells in Alex's skin sample."

"They are covering the pigment-producing melanocyte cells, clearly doing something to alter the pigment," Liz said.

"What?" Alex said. "I thought you told me there was nothing different between the two samples except for color."

She looked at him. "There wasn't."

Max glanced up from the microscope, a look of understanding on his face. "Until I came into the room."

"Exactly," Liz said. "Your presence lit them up somehow so that I could see them."

"Damn," Max said, moving back and letting Liz take up her position.

The room was silent as she studied the blue cells. There was something about them that looked familiar.

Very familiar. She just couldn't put her finger on it.

"So why would blue cells turn my skin *green*?" Alex asked.

"I have no idea why these blue cells are there," Liz said, not looking up from the blue cells. "Somehow it is changing the pigment that is being produced and spread over your skin. There's not a great distance in color between yellow and green."

"Just add blue," Alex said.

"It would seem that way," Liz said.

"So where did this blue cell come from?" Max asked.

Suddenly Max's question brought the answer to what looked familiar about the cells home. These cells were very similar to the blue stuff that had been in the cave.

"A cave," she said.

She looked around at the stunned expressions on her friends. She felt the same way. They had thought they were finished with those blue crystals when they melted, freeing Alex and Kyle from the cave a few weeks before. But now it seemed they were far from done with that adventure.

"I was wondering where all that stuff was going to go when it melted," Alex said. "We couldn't be so lucky as to have it just go away."

"No, we couldn't," Liz said.

"Figures," Maria said. She rolled her eyes, and leaned against Liz's dresser.

"It was raining that day, wasn't it?" Max asked.

"Hard," Alex confirmed.

"So the melted blue crystals were washed down into the water table," Max said.

"And right into my drinking water," Alex said.

"Mine too," Maria said. "We live close to you."

"Not only yours," Liz said, "but an entire section of the town gets their water from wells in that area."

The four of them sat there in stunned silence.

All Liz could think about was how many people had been drinking the contaminated water.

And how many of them were going to turn green before this was all over.

5

Luckily for Isabel—and everyone else in the courtyard at the hospital—the afternoon was fairly warm. She had stayed in the shade, not talking to anyone, watching new people arrive and others leave as they turned green and were taken inside. Isabel had no idea how the hospital was going to handle so many people, though thankfully the victims really didn't seem sick beyond their skin color. More than likely they were just being taken to large rooms where they, too, were just sitting around.

For the moment the new arrivals into the courtyard had slowed to a few every half hour, while those turning green seemed to have picked up speed, with some people getting upset when the skin-color change started, and others just being resigned to joining their friends and loved-ones inside.

Every so often she had checked her own skin, half expecting it to start to turn green at any moment. So far it had stayed its normal color.

Over the last hour she had tried to make a call on her

cell phone a half dozen times, with no luck. She was worried about running her cell-phone battery down, so she had forced herself not to try anywhere near as many times as she had wanted to.

As two soldiers escorted an elderly woman who was a fine shade of forest green inside the hospital, Isabel decided she needed to try again. She needed to talk to someone. And even though there were hundreds around her, she didn't dare say anything to any of them.

This time, instead of the "all circuits busy" recording, a phone on the other side rang. For a moment she couldn't even remember what number she had dialed, she was so surprised.

Then Michael answered in his gruff voice. "Crash-down."

"Michael, it's Isabel," she said, trying to keep her voice low enough that others around her wouldn't hear. Only one couple glanced toward her, then looked away.

"You all right?" he asked, clearly happy to hear from her. "We've been worrying about what happened to you."

"I'm trapped in the quarantine at the hospital."

"Oh, no," Michael said. "You're not green, are you?"

"Not yet," Isabel said. "Although I think it might only be a matter of time."

"Why?" Michael asked.

"People are dropping like flies," she said. "Although that's not the right analogy because they don't really seem sick."

"People are still turning color there?" he asked.

"Yes," she said. "Why? Aren't they doing it there?"

"There's no one in the Crashdown except the group,

and after the first wave, none of us changed. If you're not green, how'd you end up in the hospital?"

"My date turned green during the movie," Isabel said.

"Knowing the guys you go out with," Michael said, "that could be an improvement. Here's Max."

She heard him tell Max where she was and the effect she had on dates, then her brother's strong voice filled her ear. "Are you all right? Any problems?"

"I'm fine," she said. "I didn't know what else to do to calm Rob down, so I brought him here. They took him somewhere and put those of us who haven't turned green yet in a courtyard in the middle of the place."

"And you're not allowed to leave?"

"Not that I can tell," she said, glancing over at the armed guard on the nearest door. "Soldiers are keeping us locked up pretty tight. They're watching us pretty close. They're letting us go to a nearby rest-room area, but that's about all. You have any idea what's going on?"

"Actually," Max said, "Liz just discovered that the color people are turning is related to the contents of the cave."

"What cave?" she asked, just a little too loud. A lot of people turned and looked at her. Then she remembered. "Oh. Are you sure?"

"Yeah," Max said.

Isabel shook her head. She couldn't believe that these people were turning green because of the melted blue crystals in the cave from weeks earlier.

"I don't want to talk too much over the phone," Max said. "Just say that the contents of the cave went into part of the city's water supply when it melted."

"Oh, no," she said softly.

"Another problem," Max said, "is that the blue cells causing the problem can't be seen unless one of us is nearby to illuminate them."

"You're kidding," she said.

"I wish I was," Max said. "So don't go near any labs there in the hospital."

"I really wasn't planning on it," she said.

"I didn't say 'in,' Isabel," Max said. "I said 'near.'"

She froze, then looked around the courtyard. There was no way to tell if any windows looking down on her was a lab.

"How close do I have to be?" she asked.

"Pretty close. I was in the room when Liz saw the change, but it went away as I walked into the hall."

"Thank God for that," Isabel said. She would probably be all right in the courtyard then. But if the army happened to take her into a lab and noticed her presence could show cells in other's people's bodies, they would start tests on her in a heartbeat.

"Get out of there as soon as you can."

"Believe me, Max, I would if I could," she whispered, staring at the elderly couple closest to her. They didn't seem to be hearing anything.

She glanced around behind her to make sure no one was there, either. She was clear, unless someone was tapping the cell phone conversation, and she couldn't imagine why anyone would do that at this point. They were too busy gathering green people to monitor the airways.

Isabel suddenly processed what Max had said about his presence illuminating the blue cells. "How are the doctors going to be able to find a cure for this if they can't see the problem that's causing it?"

Max was silent for a long moment, then said, "I don't **know**."

Again silence.

"What should I do?" she asked, glancing around once more to make sure no one was watching. They weren't. Everyone's attention was focused across the courtyard where a woman starting to turn green was getting hysterical, fighting and shouting at a man trying to keep her calm and lead her toward a door.

Two guards rushed to her, and within a few seconds had her headed through the door, protesting every step of the way. Clearly some people did not handle situations like this well. Isabel had been in more dangerous situations than this one, but she was still amazed she was as calm as she was.

"Just stay out of everyone's way," Max said.

"That's not a problem," she said. "At least at the moment."

"I don't know how we'd get you out of there, but if we can figure out a way, we'll try. Let's hope we don't have to."

"Thanks," she said.

"Are you sure you're all right?" Max asked.

"For now I'm fine. Just tell Mom and Dad where I am."

"I will," Max said. "Call me if anything happens."

"If I can get through," Isabel said.

"Yeah," Max said after a moment. "Take care."

"You too," she said.

The line went dead, and again she felt very alone in the crowd filling the middle of the hospital in the middle of the city.

* * *

It took Max a few minutes to tell the rest of the group where Isabel was. Then he went down into the back room of the restaurant to call home to let his mom know that they were both all right. Luckily, so were his parents. No color change.

But after the phone call his stomach didn't let him believe his own lie to his mother. They were far from all right. Isabel was in the middle of a military-run quarantine, the worst place an alien in hiding could be, and the reason people were turning green was because of alien cells.

Somehow, he needed to get Isabel out of that hospital, but he had no idea how to go about that, any more than he had any idea how to stop the spread of the alien cells and turn people back to their normal colors.

He came out of the back room of the Crashdown just as Michael headed for the stairs with a glass of water filled from the counter sink.

"What are you doing?" Max asked, following him.

"Testing the water from the different taps," Michael said. "Just to make sure the Crashdown water is clean."

"Good idea," Max said. "Has it been so far?"

"One hundred percent pure city water," Michael said. "No alien cells."

Upstairs Max watched as Liz put a drop of the water from the glass on a slide and studied it. After a moment she said, "Clean."

"For the moment," Tess said from where she was standing near the window. "We don't know if those cells will spread to the water supply."

"She's right, we don't," Max said.

"I'm not really caring about water right now," Maria said. "Or where it drips or flows. How about finding a way to get these cells out of my body?"

No one said a word. Max had nothing he could say.

"The silence is sure encouraging," Alex said.

"Since I can see the cells," Liz said, "I'll try working on it. But somehow we're going to have to tell the scientists how to see the problem cells."

She looked at Max.

He knew she was right, but like the other problems, he had no idea how to go about that without blowing their cover.

"Thanks for trying," Maria said to Liz. "You'd think by now I'd start getting used to this color, but it isn't happening. It clashes with everything."

"Only you would think about fashion at a time like this," Alex said.

Maria frowned at him. "If there's a chance I'm going to be this color for some time, what else is there to think about?"

"And that's what I like about you," Michael said, next to Maria. "Knowing how to get to the real problems."

"In the meantime," Max said, trying to break up the coming argument, "we need water-table maps."

"Library," Liz said.

"They aren't on the Internet?" Alex asked.

"No," Liz said. "There are certain things governments don't put on the Internet, believe it or not."

"Because they're afraid someone'll tamper with the water supply," Michael said.

"I guess." Liz sighed. "Just not like this."

Max glanced around the group. Alex and Maria had to stay hidden since they were green. And he wanted Liz working to see if she could find something to solve the blue-cell problem. So that left him and Michael and Tess to do all the legwork.

"Looks like we're going to the library," Max said to Michael.

"Why does it take two of you to go to the library?" Alex asked.

Max smiled at Liz. "Considering everything that's going on, it might be closed."

"Oh, got it," Alex said.

Max turned to Tess. "Would you go talk to Sheriff Valenti? Tell him what we know so far, and ask him to come here. I think we're going to need his help as well, maybe getting information to the doctors in the hospital. And tell him not drink the water."

Tess nodded. "I'll check at home first. Kyle might know where he's gone."

"Don't go near the hospital," Michael said. "We don't want two of us trapped there."

"Not a chance," Tess said. With that she headed out the door.

Max watched her go, then turned to Liz. "You need anything to help you?"

"Nothing I can think of at the moment," she said. "Except more skin from Alex."

"Not on your life," he said. "Get it from Maria."

"You big baby," Maria said.

They were still arguing when he and Michael took the stairs down into the Crashdown two at a time.

* * *

Liz spent the half hour while Michael and Max were looking for maps at the library looking through the microscope. At first she used samples of her skin next to Maria's, then she finally talked Alex into a fresh sample and put his skin cells besides the ones from Maria.

It was then that she discovered exactly what she had been afraid she might find.

She had learned in class that the thin, top section of the human skin called the epidermis includes a thin, protective layer of mostly dead cells that flake off when rubbed or scraped.

The next layer are the more active cells, and the lower layer of the epidermis is where the few melanocyte pigment-producing cells were, sending the color up into the second layer. Human skin is constantly being replaced with new cell formation as the older cells die and move to the top layer to be flaked off.

And that includes the melanocyte cells, both the ones that create the skin color and the ones at the bottom of the hair follicles that create hair color.

Comparing the samples from her two friends, Liz noted that Alex's melanocyte cells had adapted more than Maria's cells. In Alex, new cells were forming a tighter and more permanent bond with the alien blue cell.

"Any luck?" Max said as he and Michael came back in. Michael was carrying a rolled-up map that Liz knew wasn't allowed to be checked out of the library. She would make sure it got back after this was all over.

"She hasn't said a word since she tortured me fifteen minutes ago," Alex said.

Max moved over to where Liz sat. "You don't look like you have good news."

"I'm not sure yet," Liz said.

"About what?" Michael asked.

"Well, first off," Liz said, "on the last scraping of skin from Maria, I got deep enough to get some hair follicles. The color-producing cells there are also covered with the blue cells, or at least they were green in color. I can make sure now that you are here."

"You mean my hair is going to turn green, too?" Maria demanded.

"It does seem like it's going to spread to your hair too," Liz said, giving her friend a weak smile and shrugging. "Sorry."

Michael snorted.

"Not funny, alien boy," Maria said, glaring at him.

"But that's not the only problem I'm seeing," Liz said. "Now that we've got Max here, let me check it one more time."

Max nodded.

Liz went back to staring at the two samples of skin under her microscope. Alex had turned green before Maria, and now that the blue cells were visible with Max and Michael nearby, it was clear. As the cells reproduced in the skin, the bond between the alien cell and the pigment-producing human cells became permanent.

She looked up at Max, then at Maria and Alex.

"Spit it out, girl," Maria said. "My skin's green, my hair's about to turn green. I can take it."

"The human body replaces its surface layer of skin every fifteen to thirty days," Liz said.

"So we have to wait that long to get back to normal color?" Alex asked. "I suppose it could be worse."

Liz shook her head.

"Worse?" Maria asked.

Liz nodded. "The alien cells seem to be bonding permanently with the new pigment-producing cells being produced, altering them in some fashion."

The silence in the room was powerful and heavy. Liz could feel the weight of the knowledge pounding down on her friends like a hammer.

"I might be wrong," she said softly. But she knew she wasn't.

"And if you're not," Max said, "how long until this change is permanent?"

"It's starting now," she said. "The skin cells are being replaced every minute of every day."

"So every hour, every day that we wait is going to make this harder to change," Max said, his gaze staring at the floor and not at her.

She knew the pressure this put him under and the decisions he was going to have to make shortly, and she didn't like it any more than he did.

"Are you telling me that if we don't find an answer soon," Maria said, standing and looking directly at Liz, "that I'm going to be green skinned, with green hair, the rest of my life?"

"This is not funny," Alex said. "Not one bit."

"No kidding," Maria said, the anger right at the surface of her words.

Max glanced up at her, then at Alex. "We'll find an answer before that happens."

"Yeah, right," Alex said, "with a high-school science student and a home microscope."

"If we have to give information to the scientists at the hospital and the base, we'll find a way to do that," Max said.

"And expose us?" Michael asked.

Max glanced at Michael, then looked at Liz. "We'll do what we have to do to reverse this."

The meaning of that statement again dropped the room into a deep, pressure-filled silence. Liz knew Max was telling the truth. If he had to risk himself and their cover to stop this, he would. She knew that. But first they needed to try to solve it on their own.

"Give me a chance first," Liz said. "I need a skin sample from you, Max. And some blood."

He nodded and sat down on the bed beside Alex, rolling up his sleeve.

"Oh, this is going to hurt you more than it does me," Alex said, smiling at Max.

"I'm not done with you yet, mister," Liz said, smiling at her tall, green friend. "And if you're not careful with Max, next time I'm going to find a really tender spot."

"Not funny," Alex said.

"There's nothing funny about this," Maria said, again sitting at Liz's dressing table and staring into the mirror. "Green hair is so last decade."

6

Outside Liz's bedroom window, the evening was slowly fading into a beautiful spring sunset. She had started out the day worrying about her job and how she could avoid Max. She had known that he wanted to have a talk about their relationship, and she wanted to avoid it. Ever since Future Max had shown up warning her about the apocalypse, she'd been trying to keep her distance, but it had been hard.

Most of her so wanted things to return to normal with him, to have a special relationship between her and Max. But every time that started, the Max from the future's words seemed to break in, haunting her. And with everything going on lately, and the arrival of Tess, they just hadn't spent much time together.

Not as much as she had wanted, which was why she had agreed to spend time with him tonight when he had asked. But that was before everything went crazy and people started turning bright green.

Now it looked that unless she found something to solve

this problem quickly, her two best friends were going to be green-skinned for the rest of their lives. And they'd have a lot of company in Roswell.

And if she couldn't find an answer, then Max might have to figure out a way to tip off the medical specialists at the hospital about the presence of the alien cell. And that would jeopardize his safety, as well as Tess and Michael and Isabel's.

Everything about this day had just turned bad.

Now Michael had gone back downstairs and Tess hadn't returned yet with Sheriff Valenti. Max had the map of the area water table spread out on the floor and was studying it.

Maria had her head down on the dressing table, her eyes shut. "I'm going to open my eyes and this will have all been a nightmare," she said.

Liz watched as Maria opened her eyes slowly and stared right at her green-skinned arm. "I'm still asleep." She snapped her eyes closed.

"I wish I was," Alex said, his leg bouncing in a nervous habit he had picked up lately. He lay back on the bed, his leg thumping, not stopping.

Liz went back to studying the skin samples under her microscope. She had put Max's on the left, and Maria's on the right. With Max in the room, the blue cells were illuminated in Maria's green skin. It was clear that the alien cells were bonding deeper and deeper with the human cells, and in just this sample alone there were a few new pigment-producing cells that looked like a permanent combination of the melanocyte cell and the alien blue cell. That wasn't a good sign at all.

"Max, could you go downstairs for a few minutes?" Liz asked. "I want to test to see if your blood illuminates the cells."

Max nodded, rolled up the map of the water tables, and headed out the door.

She waited until he was down the stairs, then pulled the slide out of the microscope and, keeping her hand braced against the edge of a book, she used a pin tip that she had dipped into Max's blood sample to touch Maria's skin sample. It left only a tiny red dot.

She quickly put the slide back into position and studied it. Her first thought was success. She could see the blue alien cells with just a little of Max's blood on the slide.

Then it dawned on her what else she was seeing. In all her days of science classes and staring through microscopes at cells, she had never imagined she would ever witness what she was seeing at that moment. A few cells in Max's blood were being drawn actively, like magnets, to the blue cells in Maria's skin.

They were pushing other skin cells aside to get there, and when Max's cells finally reached the blue alien cell, they broke the blue cell apart on contact, leaving the normal human melanocyte cell.

And then the same cells seemed to be drawn to the next closest alien blue cell, which also was broken apart.

"Amazing," she said softly.

When she had put Max's blood with the skin sample, it was only in hopes that it would light up the blue alien cells. That way she had hoped they could just anonymously give some blood samples to the doctors at the hospital to help them find a cure.

She had never expected to have this happen.

Within fifteen seconds the blue cells in the entire skin sample were gone completely, including the ones that she had thought would be permanent.

She looked up at Maria, head still down on the dressing table, then over at Alex on the bed. Could it be possible that Max's blood was the cure?

She studied the skin sample again. There wasn't a sign of blue alien cells anywhere. She stood and went to the top of the stairs. "Max, come back up for a minute."

"Okay!" Max shouted from below.

"Man," Michael's voice also floated up. "You sure let that woman boss you around."

"Right now she's the only one who has any clue what's going on." Max's voice was coming closer.

"Yeah," Michael said as faintly as before. "And it's going to get us all in trouble. Or maybe even killed. People can stay green, Maxwell."

"What if it has other effects, Michael?"

"You're going to do the hero thing again, aren't you?" Michael asked.

"Max!" Liz called out again, wanting this discussion to end.

"Only if it's necessary, Michael," Max said.

"Yeah," Michael said, "but your definition of necessary is much broader than mine."

Liz sighed. She hoped Michael would reconsider that opinion. After all, Maria was one of the people who had turned green. And no matter what he said, he really cared about Maria.

Liz went back in and sat down, again studying the skin

sample. It was as she had left it, looking normally human. No alien cells at all.

"What did you discover?" Max asked as he entered the room. For a moment she kept her eyes locked on the microscope to see if any blue cells appeared when he was close by.

Nothing.

Great!

She looked up from the microscope. "I need you to watch something."

"What?" Alex asked, sitting up and scooting to the edge of the bed with interest. "Did you find something?"

"Maybe," Liz said.

"Well, tell me when you can turn me purple," Maria said, standing. "I'll be locked in the bathroom, sobbing."

She headed out and down the hallway, but Liz was too busy to try to stop her. She took out the slide she had been studying and slipped in the slide with Alex's skin sample on it. She quickly adjusted it, made sure the blue alien cells were clearly visible, and then scooted back and pointed for Max to look.

He leaned in and stared at the slide, then nodded and stepped back, a puzzled frown on his face. "I don't see anything different from before."

"I know," she said. "But wait a minute."

She took the slide with Alex's skin sample, touched a pin-tip amount of Max's blood to one edge, and slid it back into position. She made sure it was focused, watching the cells in Max's blood attack the blue cells, then slid back for Max to take her position.

"Now look."

He again leaned forward, putting his eyes against the microscope. After a moment his body got tense as he watched what was happening.

"Would someone please tell me what's going on?" Alex asked. "This is driving me nuts."

Max stepped back, a look of excitement in his eyes, a smile covering his face. "Take a look," he said.

Alex moved off the bed and leaned over the microscope, careful not to touch or bump anything.

Max just smiled at Liz and said nothing.

Liz couldn't help but smile back. Maybe, just maybe, they had found some kind of solution to the problem. But the solution was Max's blood, and that brought up an entire new set of issues and problems.

"Wow!" Alex said, turning and looking at Liz. "Tell me what I just saw is Max's blood cells destroying the blue alien cells on contact?"

"That's what it looks like to me," Liz said, smiling at the excitement on her green friend's face.

"How?" Alex asked.

"I have no idea," Liz said. "Something in Max's blood that makes him immune to the material from the cave. That immunity attacks and destroys the invading cells."

"So now what?" Max asked.

"I suppose we need to test it," Liz said.

Max nodded and turned to look at Alex.

"You need a volunteer?" Alex said, his green hand and arm shooting in the air like he wanted to answer a question in class. "Let me be the first to stand in line, raise my hand, whatever."

Liz nodded. "You all right with this, Max?"

"I think so," Max said. "Anything to solve this problem."

Liz nodded. They needed to figure out if this was going to work, then deal with the problems of the cure being blood from the aliens later.

"Get a large glass of water from downstairs," she said to Max. "And a pitcher of water as well."

Max nodded and ran for the stairs.

She picked up the small tube of Max's blood she had collected from him earlier and looked at it. "I think we need to test the skin method first."

Alex held out his arm. "Drop it on here."

Liz shook her head. "No, I want to dilute the blood in water first. I want to find out how little of Max's blood this is going to take. We'll work up to a full drop of blood on the skin if we have to."

"Makes sense to me," he said. "From the way those cells were attacking on the microscope slide, it might not take many."

"That's my hope,"

Max came back with Michael following him. Max had the glass of water, Michael the pitcher of water.

"So," Michael said. "Is it true? Max's blood is all powerful?"

"Let's hope," Liz said.

Max handed her the glass, and she carefully dropped in one very tiny drop of Max's blood. Just about as much as she had put on the slide.

"You think that's going to be enough?" Max asked.

"I'm still not buying that your blood is the cure," Michael said.

"We don't know for sure that it is yet," Liz said. "That's what we're testing."

Michael only shrugged. "I'll believe it when I see it."

She stirred the glass of water with a pencil end. She had put so little of the blood in it, the water wasn't even pink. Maybe she should put more in?

She stared at the perfectly clear-looking water. No. She needed to start as light as possible and see how strong the attraction of Max's blood cells were to the alien cells. She knew that in that tiny pin drop there were thousands and thousands of cells. Now she had to test if just a few thousand cells in a few drops would make a difference on a body full of hundreds of thousands of blue cells replicating.

"Ready, Alex?" she asked.

He nodded. "This can't hurt worse than taking the skin samples."

"We don't know that," Max said, with mock-seriousness.

"Not funny," Alex said, holding out his arm.

Liz took the end of the pencil she had used to stir the glass, dipped it in the treated water, and pulled it out and let a few drops land on Alex's arm.

"That's it?" he asked, staring at the three or four drops on his green skin.

"More than likely we're going to need more," Liz said, "but let's just wait and see, shall we?"

"Better to test from weak to strong than the other way," Max said.

"Especially when it's your blood we're talking about," Michael said.

Liz couldn't tell if he was serious about that or not.

"So if this works," Alex said, staring at the water drops on his arm, "what should I expect?"

Liz shrugged. "I honestly don't know. The alien cells caused a change in the pigment-producing cells in your skin. If those alien cells are destroyed, it's going to take a while for the new pigment to be produced and replace the green."

"It didn't take long for me to turn green," Alex said. "Remember?"

"Not once the process started," Liz said. "That's true. But when did you take a drink of water this morning?"

"Right before I came into the restaurant," Alex said. "Maybe an hour at most before my color changed."

"Then this might take that long as well," Liz said. "Or maybe a lot longer."

"Or maybe not at all," Michael said.

Liz nodded. "Maybe."

She was starting to doubt doing the test with only a few drops at first. Maybe it would have been smarter to try the first one full dose and not wait. Now only time would tell.

7

After a few hours, Isabel decided that sitting under a tree and watching people turn green was getting old. She was stunned at how many normal-colored people had changed while she had been locked in the courtyard with them. The number here was now half of when she came in, and they were still showing no sign of letting anyone go.

Around the place people tended to sit away from anyone else. She was doing the same thing, but not because she was afraid of turning green.

She moved over toward a wall of windows that looked into a hallway that connected two buildings and formed part of one side of the enclosed courtyard. The hallway was wide enough for some benches and indoor plants, and the windows on the other side looked out at a parking lot.

Cars jammed the parking lot, and as Isabel watched, three army trucks pulled up. A few moments later, under heavy guard, a line of people with green skin were escorted out of the hospital and loaded into the trucks.

Isabel was stunned at what she was seeing. At least a hundred people were put in the trucks and then driven off. Clearly the hospital had gotten too small to hold everyone who was having a problem. But where were those people being taken?

She pulled her cell phone out of her purse and moved to a place as far from a door as she could get. A man wearing a golf shirt and slacks and golf shoes sat on a bench, talking with two other men. From the sounds of their conversation, they had each brought someone different here, and were now comparing notes. She wondered what they would do if they knew that their loved ones might have just been trucked away from the hospital.

Isabel found a spot against the wall of the building, looking back at the courtyard. There she could talk and make sure she wasn't overheard. It took three tries, but she finally got through to the Crashdown.

Again Michael answered the phone.

"Are you still all right?" he asked the moment she said hi.

"I'm fine, so far," she said. "Is Max there?"

"Yeah," Michael said. "Hold on, he's got some news for you."

"And I've got some for him," she said.

A moment later her brother came on the phone, and again she had to reassure him she was fine.

"They're not messing with you?" he asked.

"No one's even noticed me," she whispered. "But people keep turning green here."

Max sighed. "I guess that's not a surprise, given the hospital's location."

"What?"

"Never mind. I'll brief you later."

She nodded. She was walking with the phone so that no one could overhear. "Michael said you had news."

"Yeah, and it's pretty important." Max sounded excited for the first time all day.

"Well?" Isabel asked. He could be so annoying sometimes.

"Liz found out my blood cells attack the blue alien cells," he said. "We're testing it right now on Alex."

"Testing it?" Isabel asked.

"My blood, thinned in water," Max said.

"You're transfusing your blood into Alex's? That's what you're doing? That can't be safe. People can't do that with each other's, let alone ours."

A couple looked over at her. Isabel gave them a fake smile.

"No, no," Max said. "We know better than that. We're trying something else."

"What?" She suddenly needed to know everything. She didn't want them to endanger Alex at all. She cared a lot more for him than she often wanted to admit to herself.

"A few drops on the skin a few minutes ago," Max said.

"That doesn't sound healthy, either," she said. "Be careful."

"We are, as much as we can be," Max said.

Isabel always knew what that meant when her brother said it. He was in the *we-need-to-take-chances-to-solve-the-problem* frame of mind. And there was no going slow when he was like that. "Staying green would be much worse for him at this point." Max continued.

"Why? Is he getting sick?"

"No," Max said. "But I'm really worried about the army presence."

"You should be." Isabel walked as far away from people as she could. "It's getting bad here."

"In what way?"

"They're **taking** people away, Max. I just saw them drive three **truckloads** of green-skinned people away from here."

"Oh, no," Max said, his voice soft. "In army trucks."

"Yeah," Isabel said.

"Great," Max said dryly. "We possibly solve one problem and another one crops up."

A man walked past. He'd been watching her all along. She would have worried about it, except that she had seen him arrive with a green boy.

The man was just flirting with her. She turned her back on him.

"Do you think you can find out where they're going?" Max asked.

"I'm trapped in a courtyard, Max," she whispered. "Why?"

"Because if this cure works, we have to find a way to quickly get it to everyone affected. And that's going to be hard if the army has them locked up somewhere."

"If people are getting cured here, won't they bring the others back? Can't we just wait? When they return, we'll get the cure to them and—you know."

She stopped because a couple strolled past, trying to look calm.

"It won't work that way, Isabel," Max said.

"Why not?" Isabel asked, not really sure she wanted to

know the answer.

"Because Liz is pretty sure the change to green skin will become permanent in a very short amount of time. Maybe even a day."

"Oh no," was all Isabel could say.

Across the courtyard a man in jeans and a plaid shirt looked at his arms and shook his head. Then, as if accepting his fate, he stood and headed for the door. In the evening light he didn't look green to her, but more than likely he was turning and knew it.

"So anything else happening there?" Max asked.

"Nothing," she said. "We've been promised food, but so far nothing but water, coffee, and some snacks. They're going to have to take us inside somewhere pretty soon, because the air is starting to chill down."

"Keep me informed as to where they move you," Max said. "And if anything changes."

"I will," she said. "What are you planning?"

"We've got maps of the water table around the cave," he said. "And which part of the city's water supply comes from there. What we do with that information is going to depend on how the cure works, or if it even does."

"Okay. I'll call you," she said, "if anything changes here."

"Good," Max said. "You be careful and do everything in your power to stay out of the testing areas."

"I understand," she said. "Don't worry."

As she said that she pushed off from the wall and headed back into the middle of the courtyard. Until he had reminded her, she hadn't thought that the lab areas might be right behind the wall she had been leaning against.

"Be careful," he said.

"You too," she said, and clicked her phone closed.

She moved over the bench where the man who had just turned green had been sitting. It was still in the sun and fairly warm. Luckily she had taken a sweater to the movie, but a sweater wasn't going to keep her warm on a high desert spring night in early March. Not even close.

But at the same time, she didn't want to be moved to some other unknown location. Not yet at least.

At that moment, on the far side of the courtyard, near the door she had come in, a metal door opened exposing a kitchen beyond. A man with an apron stood in the door. "Dinner through here!" he shouted, loud enough for everyone in the courtyard to hear.

The talking around her got louder as people slowly moved, standing, stretching, saying something to their neighbors.

Isabel stood as well and walked slowly toward the door, falling in line behind a man and a young girl. Finally there was something to do, even if it was only eating dinner. It was a lot better than sitting and waiting to turn green.

"Hey!" Alex shouted. "Look at this!"

"Max!" Liz called out a few moments later.

Max had just hung up the phone in the back room of the Crashdown and was moving through the door to talk to Michael, who was sitting at the counter drinking a soda and reading the paper as if nothing was happening. Even though no one had bothered to change the restaurant's

OPEN sign to CLOSED, no customers had come through the door since the last two had run away earlier.

The shout from Alex and Liz now sent Max running up the stairs toward Liz's bedroom, with Michael right behind him.

"You all right?" he asked as he burst into her room.

"All right?" Alex said, his green face beaming. "You tell me." He held out the arm Liz had put the water drops on. A huge area of normal-colored skin was spreading from the water drops, one line going toward his fingers, the other moving toward his shoulder.

"Can you feel that?" Liz asked.

"No," Alex said as they all watched the line between green skin and regular skin move.

"How can it be acting so fast?" Max asked, completely stunned at what he was seeing.

"I don't know, exactly," Liz said. "I may have been wrong about the pigment produced by the cells actually changing color."

"How would that work then?" Alex asked as the color line reached his wrist, making his arm look very strange with regular skin and a green-skinned hand.

"I honestly don't know," Liz said. "I suppose the green could have been completely caused by the blue cells changing the light reflected from the natural pigment to look green."

Max stared at Alex's arm as the human teen slipped off his shirt to follow the transformation process. The line of green skin was being pushed up onto his shoulder, and seemed to be slowing some as it moved over his chest and around his neck. Max figured the slowing was from fewer of his cells attacking a larger area of Alex's skin surface.

"You look like someone's idea of a bad movie monster," Michael said.

"The man with the two-toned skin," Alex said, flexing his muscles.

Liz laughed. "Don't try leaping any tall buildings just yet."

Max had to admit it was the strangest thing he had seen in a long time. Over half of Alex's chest, one arm, and most of his face was still a pretty bright green. The rest of him looked normal-skinned and pale from no suntan.

"That's not my super power," Alex said, pretending to be insulted. "Down on the street they call me the Two-toned Kid."

"I wouldn't be admitting that name," Michael said.

"Anyone home?"

The shout from Sheriff Valenti echoed up from the restaurant.

"Up here!" Max shouted. "Hurry!"

"You don't want to miss this show," Michael said, shaking his head as the line of green to normal skin moved up over Alex's nose and across his chest toward his left arm.

"I could always take my pants off," Alex said.

"Not in my bedroom," Liz said, laughing.

"Especially when you're still green," Michael said. "She likes her men a little riper."

Liz glared at Michael as Tess and Sheriff Valenti came in. Both of them stopped and stared at Alex, clearly stunned at the two-toned kid.

"I feel like a sideshow freak in a circus," Alex said, laughing as one color line reached his shoulder and started down his green arm, picking up speed, while the other line disappeared into his hairline on his forehead.

"You look like one at the moment," Max said.

"What's happening?" Valenti asked. "How did you do this?"

"Liz discovered that the infected people had blue cells attached to their pigment cells in their skin. Blue cells from the cave."

"Oh," Valenti said, nodding, suddenly understanding. "When the stuff melted it went down into the water table."

"Exactly," Max said. "And when people drank it, or showered in the water, it attached to the pigment-producing cells in our body, causing people to turn green. And when Liz discovered my blood destroyed the blue cells, we decided to test it on Alex."

"Your blood?" Valenti asked.

"You're kidding, right?" Tess asked.

Max shook his head. He wished he were kidding, but at this point just having a solution made him happy.

"I discovered it by accident," Liz said. She held up a glass of water. "We put a tiny drop of Max's blood in this, and then I put just two drops of this water on Alex ten minutes ago."

"And it did this?" Valenti said, pointing to Alex.

"The Green Fist lives!" Alex said, holding up his green fist as the color line reached his wrist.

"For about ten seconds," Michael said. "Then it's going to be the green finger."

"Let's hope it doesn't stop there," Alex said, smiling.

"It's not going to stop," Liz said. "If it does, we cut the finger off."

Max and everyone else laughed.

"Oh, come on, little Max cells," Alex said, holding his hand up as the green skin area got smaller and smaller, "keep on fighting the good fight."

Max was amazed. Two seconds later Alex appeared to be completely back to normal.

"Okay, pale-skinned boy," Liz said to Alex, "I need a skin sample."

"Now, wait," Alex said, "that hurts."

"Quit whining and just be glad you're not green," Liz said, smiling at him. "Max is giving his blood, you can donate a little more skin."

"All right," he said, holding out his arm for her to take another small sample. "But not too deep."

"So this cures the problem if the water with Max's blood in it touches someone who is green," Valenti said. "How about drinking the water?"

"We still have Maria to test that on," Michael said. "Put a little in a glass and I'll give it to her without telling her what it might do."

Max dumped the glass of water with his small drop of blood in it into the pitcher of water, then poured out about a half glass. "Is that about right?" he asked Liz.

"You can't even tell there's anything in that," Tess said.

"There's enough," Liz said, "if Max's cells make it through the digestive system of the body. The blue alien cells did, it seems, so I think his will as well."

She finished taking the skin sample from Alex and Max, and the rest watched as she put it on a slide and checked it under the microscope. After a moment she turned, smiling. "Normal as your skin will ever be," she said, smiling at Alex.

"All right," Michael said, taking the glass of water. "Let's try it this way with sulking green girl in the bathroom."

He headed off down the hallway, and a moment later the sound of knocking on the bathroom door filled the hallway. If anyone could get Maria to drink some water, it was Michael, of that much Max was sure.

"Let's assume this is going to work both ways," Valenti said. "How do we get this to the doctors at the hospital to give to the infected?"

Max stared at him, not really sure what he was saying.

"We don't," Tess said. "We fix this ourselves."

Max nodded. As far as he could see, fixing this now, tonight, was the only choice they had.

"Tess is right," Liz said. "We can't take samples of Max's blood to the hospital because they'd know it was alien. And if we don't act fast, some of this change of color might become permanent."

"Permanent?" Both Valenti and Tess asked at the same moment.

Liz quickly explained to them what she had found, and that to be safe, they had to get this problem solved in the next twenty-four hours. The sooner, the better.

"We have another problem," Max said. "I just spoke to Isabel from the quarantine area at the hospital. She saw the army taking a hundred or so green-skinned people away in trucks."

"Figures," Valenti said.

"And that's not counting all the people like Kyle staying home, even though their skin is green," Tess said. "How are we going to reach all of them with drops of Max's blood?"

The silence in the room was so loud Max wanted to say something just to break it. But there just wasn't an answer to Tess's question that he could figure out. But for the sake of a lot of people, he had to figure out something soon.

8

The sun had almost set outside Liz's bedroom window, the warm spring weekend now a memory. The day sure hadn't turned out like Liz had hoped, but this year they seldom had. And tomorrow she had to be back in school. That was going be hard, at best. Maybe even impossible. From all she knew, the health officials might even cancel school tomorrow if this green-skinned problem didn't get solved. If it didn't, Roswell, New Mexico, was going to be famous very soon for a lot more than a flying saucer crash decades before.

But right now Liz was worried about something very important, but she didn't quite know how to bring up the subject. Maybe jumping right in would be the way.

"Okay," Liz said, looking around at Sheriff Valenti, Tess, Max, and the newly recovered Alex, "I'm having some ethical problems with using Max's blood like this without doing real testing on it."

She took a deep breath and went on. "I don't think Alex or Maria minds dealing with Max's blood. But I don't think we should expose a large number of people to another alien substance without taking some precautions first. No matter how good our intent and reasons are."

She let out the breath and looked into Max's eyes. Clearly he was agreeing with her.

"You saying Max might have some sort of alien disease?" Tess asked.

"I just think we're a lot better off being safe," Liz said, "rather than sorry later, pardon the cliché."

"So what kind of precautions are you talking about?" Valenti asked.

"The same kind the Red Cross would use when taking and distributing blood," Liz said. "I want to do some basic tests, at least."

"If my blood is reduced to plasma, will it have the same effect on the alien blue cells?" Max asked.

"It might," Liz said, smiling at him. He was already thinking along the same lines she was. "But we'd have to make sure by finding a test subject."

"The high school has a machine in the lab that can reduce blood down to plasma," Max said. "And enough equipment there in the lab to do some basic tests."

"Exactly," Liz said. "I'm going to feel a lot better about trying this cure on a large number of people if we take some precautions first. Spreading blood around these days is just too dangerous, even when we know where the blood comes from."

Tess nodded. "I agree."

"So do I," Valenti said. "Good thinking."

Liz was very glad they all did agree. She wasn't sure why she thought they might not. But in this instance, taking the extra time to make sure Max's blood was as safe as possible might save a major problem later, something that none of them dared think about happening.

Down the hall the bathroom door opened and closed, and Michael came back into the bedroom.

"Well?" Max asked.

Michael held up the empty glass. "Got her to drink it a couple of minutes ago, but she's not a happy person, I can tell you that. And no sign of change in skin color when I left."

"Why didn't you tell her what you were trying?" Valenti asked.

"No point," Michael said. "If it fails, we'll cure her the same way Liz did Alex. No point in making her more unhappy in the process."

"Would you be happy if your skin was green?" Liz asked.

"I wasn't," Alex said, "especially knowing it might be permanent."

"I'm an alien among humans," Michael said, holding Liz's gaze. "If my only problem was having green skin, it would be a relief."

Tess laughed. "You got that right."

Liz saw that Max was nodding as well. At times like this she wondered how hard it really was to be one of the four of them. It was tough enough just being their friends.

"Besides," Valenti said, "people with different-colored skins live perfectly normal lives in this country."

Liz didn't want to get into a racial discussion with the sheriff, so she said nothing. And clearly neither did any of the others.

"Yes, but how many people do you know who happen to be green?" Michael asked.

"And if folks think the green is caused by a disease, that could be really bad," Tess said.

"I don't like it." Michael shook his head. "Roswell has enough troubles without being the place where little green men originated."

"I think most people already consider it that," Liz said.

"Oh, yeah," Michael said. "That's why my life is so hard."

"So," Max said loudly, clearly trying to stop the sidetrack, "if this works and assuming we can use my blood plasma, how are we going to get it to the people who need it?"

"We dump some of the cure into the cave," Michael said. "I assume your cells would attack the blue cells in the water as well as in human skin."

"We can test that," Liz said, thinking about how they just needed to find some contaminated water. More than likely the water at Valenti's house was inside the contaminated area, since Kyle had turned green. She had no idea why the sheriff hadn't. Maybe hadn't taken a drink of water—or a shower—this morning.

"If Michael's right," Tess said, "and Max's plasma cells work as well as his normal blood cells, the water table should contain the cure for some time."

"Allowing people to drink it in their own homes," Max said. "Perfect."

"A lot of *ifs* between now and then," Valenti said. "Not counting the problem of even getting enough of it in the cave to go down into the water table."

"That's right," Alex said. "It's not raining today."

Silence filled the room. Liz was starting to see even more problems than she had first suspected. Making certain Max's blood safe was the least of them.

"Wow! Wow! Wow!"

The shout from the bathroom echoed through the entire building. A moment later Maria slammed open the door and jumped out into the hallway. From where Liz was, she could see Maria spreading out her arms.

"Look, it's gone!" she shouted, coming toward them in the bedroom. "My normal color is back! I'm pink again!"

"Pale is more like it," Michael said, just loud enough for those nearby to hear.

Maria came bursting into the room, the smile on her face so big Liz wondered if her skin might tear. Maria spent a lot more time on taking care of her looks every day than Liz did, and it was important to Maria how she looked. Liz could only imagine how awful Maria must have felt when she thought she might be green-skinned for the rest of her life.

But it was clear how relieved she was now.

"Isn't this great!" Maria said, standing with her arms out. She touched her face, her skin on her arms. "See! No green."

"Looks like that worked," Michael said.

"Alex!" Maria said, going over and giving him a hug, "you're cured, too? What happened?"

"Liz solved it," Alex said.

"What?" Maria asked, looking at Alex, his words sinking in through the excitement. She then turned to face Liz and the rest of them. "What did you find that would work? Was it in the glass of water? Why didn't you tell me?"

"It was in the water," Liz said, smiling at her friend. She

liked it when Maria was happy, and right now she was about as happy as a person could be.

"And we didn't want to tell you in case it didn't work," Michael said. "We didn't want to get your hopes up and then dash them."

Maria studied him for a moment. Liz held her breath. It seemed like everyone in the room was. They all knew this next moment could go either way. Maria could be angry that they withheld information from her, or she could be grateful that they didn't get her hopes up.

Then she smiled again.

"Thank you," she said, going over to Michael and kissing him hard on the lips. He let her, closing his eyes, and then he seemed to remember that the others were in the room. He pulled her back just enough to separate them.

"You're welcome," he said.

Maria turned around and grinned at Liz. "What did you find that would erase the green?"

Liz felt uncomfortable telling Maria what they had done, but someone had to, so she just blurted it out. "Max's blood."

"Max's blood what?" Maria asked.

"Max's blood cured you," Liz said. "A tiny drop in that pitcher of water lets his cells fight and destroy the blue alien cells in your skin that were turning it green."

"I drank Max's blood?" Maria asked, the smile fading a little on her face as she realized what Liz had told her.

Liz nodded. "Just a very tiny amount. Not enough to even color the water."

"Now I'm really green," Maria said, trying to make herself look serious. Then she shouted "Not!"

And everyone laughed. To Liz it felt great that her best friend was back to normal.

Then Maria's smile faded. "It's not going to come back, is it?"

"What?" Liz asked.

"The green," Maria said. "I'm not going to have to drink Max's blood for the rest of my life, am I?"

"No, I don't think so," Liz said.

"Oh, thank heavens," Maria said.

"Yeah," Michael said. "The last thing I wanted was to be dating Vampirella."

Maria turned toward him, her eyes twinkling. "We're dating now?"

"I didn't say that," Michael said.

"If this is a date," Alex said dryly, "it's a mighty strange one."

Liz smiled. She loved the feeling of joy in the room. But, she knew, they weren't done. "We still have some things to do," she said.

"Yeah," Max said. "And I have a funny feeling that time is running out."

Isabel's dinner was a decent-tasting piece of chicken, some canned corn, potatoes that were clearly flaked, and gravy that was so runny, it flowed over everything else. Hospital food, in other words, thickened up to almost the level of school cafeteria fare. Almost.

It took her a while to find the Tabasco sauce, though. Apparently Tabasco wasn't standard fare in a hospital cafeteria. The kindly woman who had been sharing Isabel's table asked if the Tabasco improved the taste of the food. Isabel lied and said it didn't.

After she and the rest of the prisoners were finished eating in the smallish dining area near the kitchen and the courtyard, the guards lead them toward a large theater area.

The room was big enough to hold a few hundred people in seating, and was clearly designed for teaching. Isabel didn't even know such a room existed in the hospital, but her interests had never much gone toward medicine, and she hadn't spent much time in the hospital, except with friends.

Isabel let out a small sigh. She wondered how Rob was doing. She didn't even know if he was still in the hospital. She hoped he wasn't one of the people who had been removed by the army.

She adjusted her sweater around her shoulders. At least in the big classroom it was warm, unlike out in the courtyard. Pillows and blankets were stacked on the small stage, and coffee and tea were set on a table. They were expected to sleep in the chairs, it seemed.

"Where's the rest room?" One lady right ahead of Isabel asked a guard as they were ushered into the theater.

He pointed to a side door guarded by two other soldiers and didn't say a word.

"Looks like they're setting us up to stay in here for a while," another man said.

"Planning on keeping us till we all turn green," a second man said.

Isabel figured that was about right. Anyone in this room had been near a person who turned green. So thinking that the green skin was a type or epidemic, it was no wonder they were being held in quarantine. It made sense, even for the army.

She moved across the room toward the farthest side, away from the door they had come in, then took her phone out of her purse. She had to let Max know where they had been moved. And find out what was going on there. This being cut off from the rest of the group was starting to drive her nuts.

She punched in the number of the Crashdown and pressed dial.

Just as she pushed it, her phone beeped and the low-battery signal came on.

"Oh, no, don't do that," she said aloud.

"Mine went dead two hours ago," a woman said nearby. "You have a charger?"

"No," Isabel said, still staring at her now useless cell phone. Her charger was sitting on her desk in her bedroom, where it would do her no good at all.

She stared at her dead phone for a moment longer, resisting tossing it against the concrete wall, then stuffed it back into her purse. Now how was Max going to find her?

He wasn't, that was for sure.

She looked around at the people slowly settling into seats like a class getting ready for an instructor to come in. Only this class had armed guards making sure no one skipped. Even if Max did find her, there was no way he could get her and the others out of here.

She moved up to the front of the classroom and picked up a blanket and pillow, then went back to a seat in the second row where she could curl up.

Behind her the woman whose cell phone had gone

dead hours before was stretched out, her eyes closed. And if Isabel wasn't mistaken, her skin had a sickly green tint to it.

Valenti, Max, Michael, and Liz were headed for the high school, following the same route Max took every day. Only this time it felt strange, riding in Valenti's truck, almost no traffic on the roads.

It was Sunday night. Max told himself that there never was much traffic on Sunday night, but tonight it felt isolated and very, very empty. Max figured that was his imagination, but the tension in the truck mounted as every silent block passed.

"How many people do you think have turned green?" Valenti asked, clearly just trying to break the silence.

"It can't be a large number," Michael said. "Maybe a few hundred."

"It hadn't made the news this afternoon," Liz said, "so the number must be small."

"No," Valenti said. "They wouldn't report this. The authorities would keep a quarantine quiet as long as they could."

Max frowned. He hadn't thought of that. "Wouldn't they try to keep people away from the city?"

"Sure," Valenti said. "But they can cover it with the story of a chemical spill or something. They're not going to start a public panic."

"Well, it'll start eventually," Michael said. "No matter how many people are affected. They have to start telling someone."

"Not if it's confined to a small location, and the way that

this was spreading, I have a hunch the affected area isn't that large," Valenti said.

"I agree," Max said. "The area of the city's water table fed from the forest around the cave is pretty small. Your house is in it."

Valenti grinned as he steered around a corner. "Lucky for me I didn't take a drink of water or shower this morning."

"That's what that smell is," Michael said.

Valenti just shook his head and said nothing.

Max thought about how lucky they had been so far. Roswell was a pretty large place, and if the water table from the cave area was used for the entire town, almost everyone would be green by now. But the army and doctors were treating it as a small plague of some sort. The quiet around them right now had to be normal. Unless they got this solved, it wasn't going to be quiet for long.

Valenti pulled into the parking lot.

"Let's go around back," Michael said.

Valenti nodded and focused on getting through the parking lot. Max hadn't wanted the sheriff to go along, but Valenti had insisted. "It's better that I'm there now instead of bailing you three out of jail later."

Max had agreed with the sentiment. They didn't have time to be arrested, from what Liz was saying. The longer they waited on getting a some of his blood cells into people to fight the alien blue cells, the more chance there was of people remaining green-skinned for the rest of their lives.

And more chance of the infected water spreading.

Max was still uncomfortable with having his blood cells

being the cure, but he was forcing himself to deal with it. And having the rest of the group just as uncomfortable with it helped.

Valenti pulled his truck right up behind the school and tucked it into a parking alcove that hid it from all but the most dedicated search. The school's parking lot looked strange under the lights. Max was used to seeing it filled with cars.

But Valenti seemed to know all the secret places. Which was good, since he'd been having a lot of trouble lately, mostly because of helping them, and was more often on leave from his job than he was on duty. Max hadn't talked with him about it too much, but Max knew that the last thing Valenti needed now was to get caught doing something questionable, like escorting three kids into the high school on a Sunday evening. That would be very hard to explain.

They got out of the truck and hurried toward one of the lesser-used exits. Usually, this one was off limits. The door was thick and metal, without any windows.

Max stood on the stoop and tried it. The door was locked. Liz was facing the parking lot, watching to see if anyone came by. Valenti was pressed against the building, as was Michael.

"It's yours," Max said to Michael.

Michael nodded. He unlocked the door easily using his powers and slipped inside. Max inclined his head toward Valenti, who followed Michael. Then Liz went in, and finally Max stepped through the door. He gave the parking lot one last look before easing the door shut.

The high school's familiar chalk-and-old-tennis-shoe

smell was instantly comforting. Then Max turned around and the feeling vanished. The empty halls felt almost haunted by echoes of all the voices from the students during the day. The place seemed smaller at night, and dangerous.

Michael unlocked the science room door just as easily as the outer door, and then the cabinet and storage closest containing the equipment Liz was going to need. The first thing she did was set Max up to give a pint of blood, making him lie down on a lab table.

With Michael standing guard just outside the door, and Valenti down the hallway toward the front door, the process of drawing Max's blood seemed to take forever. Neither Max or Liz spoke. There really wasn't much to say as far as he was concerned. And Liz was good and seemed to know what she was doing, or was at least pretending very well.

After she had his blood, she took a few drops and ran a few tests while he lay on the lab table and held a piece of gauze to his arm.

"What kind of tests are you running?" he asked.

"A couple we learned in class," Liz said.

He remembered those tests. He'd borrowed some of Liz's blood so that he could conduct his. "You think I have hepatitis?"

"Don't worry," she said. "I'd be shocked if you do. After all, you don't seem to get sick. I just want to be cautious."

"We don't have a lot of time, Liz."

"I know." She sighed. "It doesn't matter, anyway. Your blood is so different from ours that I can't even type it."

"Think the plasma will separate out?"

Liz nodded. "The blood looks similar to humans. It's just different in the details."

"You guys going to be done soon?" Michael asked, sticking his head in the door.

"Soon," Liz said, brushing Michael away with her hand.

He snorted and went back out into the hallway.

"Good news," she said after about five minutes of very intense, very long silence, "you're healthy, as far as I can tell."

She put the container holding his blood in a machine and clicked it on. The whirring sounded incredibly loud.

"This will separate your red blood cells from your blood plasma," Liz said. "It's the cells in the plasma that will fight the blue cells causing this."

"You're sure?" Max asked, sitting up and putting the piece of gauze he'd been holding against his arm in his pocket.

"Pretty sure," Liz said. "We'll need to test it on someone to make sure."

"Kyle," Max said.

"Sounds logical to me," Liz agreed.

"Done," she said after a few more minutes of them both standing and watching the machine in silence.

Max helped her put back the equipment and lock up the closet and cabinet, then with a quick check to make sure everything was back in the place it had been when they came in, they headed for the sheriff's truck.

Max could feel the tension among them ease as Valenti headed down the road and away from the high school. It was as if they could all breathe again.

"Let's go to your house," Max said to Valenti. "We'll test

the plasma on Kyle so he can help us with the next stage of what's going to happen."

"Kyle's not real happy right now," Valenti said. "He's not going to be excited to see you."

"Oh," Liz said, smiling, "Kyle's going to be happy enough when he knows we have the cure for what ails him."

"Let's hope," Michael said.

Max was still not sure about turning his blood into plasma, but if it did prove to work as well on Kyle as it had on Alex and Maria, then they had the next big problem: How to get his blood plasma either on the skin, or inside everyone who was infected with the blue alien cells?

No one said a word, and the ride to Valenti's house was short and silent as Max faced what seemed like an impossible task.

9

Liz finished filling a pitcher of water from the kitchen sink in Kyle and Sheriff Valenti's house. The place was certainly a lot cleaner since Tess had moved in. Liz could remember visiting before Tess had joined the Valentis, back when Liz and Kyle were dating, and the house had seemed like the quintessential bachelor's pad. Dishes would litter the sink, and there'd be crumbs all over the couch.

Now a dining table had mysteriously appeared from somewhere, along with three chairs, and the kitchen looked spotless. The faint odor of garbage no longer lingered around the place any more, either.

Liz couldn't believe that Tess was doing all the work. If she had to bet, she would wager that Tess guilted Kyle and Sheriff Valenti into keeping the house spic-and-span.

Just in the dining room Max, Michael, and Valenti were trying to cheer up Kyle, who was insisting he didn't want to even bother with any of them again. Actually, Michael and Valenti were doing most of it. Liz knew that after what had happened in the fall, or what Max thought had happened in the fall between her and Kyle, Max had not been comfortable around Kyle. Max had never said anything after his first questions, but his feelings were clear and on the surface.

"I'm tired of getting mixed up in your alien problems," Kyle said, his voice raising in anger. "Go do your lab tests on someone else."

"Can't say as I blame you," Michael said, "but right now your skin is your problem. And Liz thinks she can fix it. Do you like being as green as an avocado?"

Liz carried the pitcher back out into the dining area. "I *can* fix it, Kyle. We got Alex and Maria back to normal. It should only take a few minutes."

Then she realized that Valenti, Michael, and Max were all staring at what she had in her hand. "What?" she asked, then looked at the pitcher. It was full of a rich, blue water. It had been clear, she was certain, coming out of the tap.

"That's your cure?" Kyle asked.

"Actually," Liz said, sitting the pitcher on the table, "that came out of your tap. It looked fine until I brought it in here."

"My presence is lighting up the blue cells," Max said.

"I'm helping," Michael said.

"Looks that way," Liz said. "Same as in the skin samples. The alien cells in the water are illuminated."

"I'm not drinking that," Kyle said.

"Well, you have been," Liz said, even though she didn't exactly blame him. Blue water didn't look appetizing. It actually seemed like an odd form of Kool-Aid.

"I have not," Kyle said. "Whatever you put in there turned the water blue."

"Tell you what," Liz said, getting tired of all the male whining she'd been hearing all day. "Take this back into the kitchen and see if it stays blue."

Kyle frowned at her. "You're serious."

"Yes," she said. "I am."

"I've really been drinking that stuff?"

"And showering in it," Valenti said.

"Yeah." Michael crossed his arms and leaned back in his chair. "And it turned you as green as a leaf. We're here to fix your water and you."

Kyle looked at him, then shook his head, disgusted.

Liz dipped an eyedropper into the bag of Max's plasma and put one drop into the water pitcher. She expected a slow reaction, but not what she got. Instantly the water turned clear. The drop of Max's plasma cells cleared the blue alien cells out of the water in a fraction of a second.

Everyone stared at it in surprise.

"Well," Max said after a moment, "so much for testing to see if the stuff works in just plain water."

"*Works* would be an understatement," Michael said.

Liz poured a glass of water out of the pitcher and handed it to Kyle. "It should turn your skin back to its normal color."

"And poison me in the meantime, right?"

"Pickle Boy is not a good nickname," Michael said. "Give this a shot."

"Trust me," Liz said, looking directly into Kyle's eyes and handing him the newly refilled glass. "I'd rather have you back to normal."

"Yeah, the green's starting to glare," Michael said.

"Besides, we need your help in saving the rest of the

town," Max said, his voice serious, "and we need you back to normal to do that."

Kyle shook his head, looking first at Max, then his dad, then Liz. "All right."

He downed it in one quick drink, just as his dad had done.

A few drops spilled on his hands and down his face in the process.

"Look at that!" Michael said.

Liz was staring as the drops on Kyle's face turned his skin back to normal, then the effect started to spread, much faster than it had with Alex and Maria.

"What?" Kyle said, clearly panicked.

"Look at your hand," Liz said, smiling. "A drop from the glass landed on your hand."

Kyle held his hand up and watched as the line of green quickly moved up over his wrist and under his shirt, leaving his hand its normal color.

His other hand was still green, and he held it out just in time to see the green fade.

"Welcome back, Avocado Boy," Michael said.

Slowly a smile broke out over Kyle's face that seemed to light up the room, and in just seconds everyone was smiling right along with him.

"Thank you," Kyle said, inspecting his hands one more time, then climbing off the couch and giving Liz a hug. "Thank you, thank you, thank you."

Max watched from his place in the dining room. Liz could feel his gaze on her. She wanted to tell him that the hug meant nothing, but of course, she couldn't.

She made herself smile at Kyle. "You're more than welcome."

He eased out of the hug and looked at the entire group. "So, what do you need me to do to help?"

His mood changed so suddenly, it even surprised Liz. But then, Maria's mood had changed that quickly, too. Would Liz have been as depressed as they were about being green?

Probably.

She was just glad she didn't have a chance to find out.

Valenti patted Kyle on the back and grinned at him. Even the sheriff seemed relieved. Maybe he had been more worried than he had let on.

"Let's go back to the Crashdown and plan what to do next," Max said, turning and heading for the door.

Liz caught a glimpse of his face before he turned away. It was full of pain from seeing Kyle hug her. What she was letting him believe about her and Kyle was cruel.

But now was not the time to worry about it. Right now they had a much bigger problem that threatened the lives of a lot of people, not the least of whom were Max, Michael, Isabel, and Tess.

Maria had the CLOSED sign out when they pulled up in front of the Crashdown.

"Any call from Isabel?" Max asked as they went inside.

"Nothing," Maria said. "I tried to reach her, but couldn't get through. I can't tell if they're blocking the signal or if her phone's dead."

"Well, she's been able to call out," Max said. "Let's hope she does again."

"You'd think she would have called by now." Alex came up just behind Maria. Now that he was no longer green, he seemed even more concerned about Isabel.

He was such a nice guy. Max had no idea why Isabel kept avoiding him. Max had also noticed that no one had really told Alex that Isabel had been on a date when she went to that movie.

"Maybe she hasn't had enough privacy to call," Liz said.

"I hope that's the problem," Max said. But he didn't like the feeling of worry that was slowly growing about her situation. They needed to move and move fairly fast.

The Crashdown seemed more comfortable than the high school had been. Max didn't want to think about how many times they'd planned an important operation from here.

Liz dimmed some of the lights so that it looked like the place was closed, then helped Kyle move chairs toward the center of the room. Max didn't want a chair, especially not one that Kyle had touched.

Liz had tried to reassure him that whatever had happened with Kyle was over, but she had told him that once before. And she had looked awfully pleased when Kyle hugged her.

Max didn't meet her gaze as he spread the city water-supply map on the center table. The group sat around it, all except for Max, Kyle, and Valenti, who studied it from above while standing.

On the drive back from Valenti's house, Max had forced himself to think about the problem at hand, and not the rift between him and Liz. And now that all the testing of this cure was done, he had some ideas on how to handle it. Not many, but a few.

Around the table was the entire group. Maria leaned against Michael, Valenti and Kyle stood, their backs against the counter, Tess, Liz, and Alex sat in chairs. Only Isabel's tall and strong presence was missing.

"Okay," Max said, "I see this as a three-front attack. And from what Liz has discovered about the coloring in people's skin, we need to attack on all three fronts at the same time to make sure we get everything done in time."

Everyone nodded, but most important, Michael. Max trusted Michael's judgment on these sort of things a great deal, and right now he was going to need to listen to him if he had ideas.

"First," Max said, "we need to get a lot of water containing the cure into that cave and the water table below it."

"After what came out of our faucet," Kyle said, "I completely agree with that."

"What came out?" Maria asked.

"Blue water," Kyle said. "Full of the melted alien cells from the cave."

"Yuck," Maria said. "We drank that stuff."

Kyle grimaced. "I know."

"Anyone have any ideas," Max asked, "on how to go about getting the cure down into the water table?"

"The city has a large water truck," Valenti said, "used for hauling water for construction and cleaning streets. You dump an entire load from that down into that cave, and it's going to reach the water table."

Max nodded. That was a great idea. He turned to Liz. "Do we have enough to treat an entire water truck?"

"More than enough," Liz said. "I think a quarter of what we have for a full truck would do the job."

"So why not make sure and do two truckloads?" Michael asked. "We have enough, right?"

Liz nodded. "That we do."

"It's a safer bet," Valenti said.

"I agree," Max said. "Good. Our second front of attack is getting the cure to people in the hospital. And while we're at it, we'll get Isabel out of there."

"That's going to be difficult if not impossible," Valenti said. "The army has set up a wide perimeter around the hospital and has armed men everywhere. The city police and the sheriff's department are helping patrol."

Max nodded. "Any ideas?"

"People have to go to work there," Maria said. "I bet they're letting in medical staff."

Max smiled at her. When Maria was calm, she was a real asset to the group. "You're right. We need to check that out to make sure, but I think you might have something."

"So what about the group that was taken by the army?" Valenti asked. "We don't even know where they are."

"That's true," Max said, "and finding their location has to be our first priority. Let's head out two at a time and see what information we can find. There are only a few dozen places off the base large enough for them to be held in, and we've already checked the high school."

For the next five minutes they decided who would check which area of town, what to look for, and what to do if they found it. Then they agreed to meet back at the Crashdown after one hour.

Kyle went with his father and left first to check the base. Maria went with Michael to check the area near the hospital and find out if employees were being allowed inside the hospital. Liz and Alex went together to check some warehouses and a theater. That left Tess with Max.

Part of Max wondered if he put the groupings together in spite. Let Liz deal with him and Tess together. Or maybe he was just trying to make her jealous.

He tried not to think about it. He and Tess had to check more warehouses and the mall area. That was where his focus should be.

"One hour, people," Max said as the teams headed for the door. "Meet right back here. And be careful."

Max and Tess were the last ones out the door. He just hoped on this first mission, everyone made it back safely. It was going to take all of them to solve this problem.

All of them and a lot of luck.

10

Max waited until Kyle and the sheriff, the last two, arrived back. While he waited he sat on a stool, working on a plate of French fries that Michael had made for everyone to munch on. Alex had made himself a chocolate milkshake, and Tess had settled for Coke when it was clear that starting the coffeemaker was going to be too much trouble.

The fries were good and salty. Max had pulled a plate aside for him and Tess so that they could pour Tabasco on theirs. No matter how many times the others had seen him do that, it still grossed them out.

But he was hungry. None of them had had dinner. He was wondering if he could get Michael to cook some burgers. It might be a stretch. Michael wasn't the happiest of campers right now. Apparently searching with Maria hadn't gone as well as Max had hoped it would.

Max's search hadn't gone well, either. The warehouses and mall area were as dead as they should be on a Sunday night, and it didn't take any more than a drive past to see that.

Still, they had gotten out and looked around. Tess had a few other ideas about where to search, and Max went along with her. Even though he had kept an eye out for the army's new base, he'd found his mind wandering. He kept wishing he were with Liz instead.

He wondered if Tess could sense that. She'd seemed cranky, too, by the time they'd gotten back.

Kyle and Valenti came through the front door. As they did, Valenti grinned. His was the only positive reaction they'd had all night, and it gave Max hope.

"None of the rest of us has found anything," Max said. "Have you?"

"Yeah," Valenti said. "We found them."

Kyle nodded. "They're in one of the warehouses. We watched an army truck bring in another group."

"Warehousing people?" Tess asked and shuddered.

"They might be running out of room at the hospital," Liz said.

"Which warehouse?" Max asked.

"Just inside the army base," Valenti said.

"We got as close as we dared," Kyle said.

Valenti nodded. "From the looks of it, there are about a hundred of them in the warehouse. Everyone else is still in the hospital."

Max didn't ask how he got the information. More than likely it hadn't done his job any more good to be asking questions.

"You didn't ask me about the hospital," Maria said.

Max looked at her.

She raised her eyebrows at his surprised expression. He had to admit she did look better with her normal skin color. As she had said, green did not become her.

"You were just concerned with where the army had taken everyone," Maria said. "You forgot that I was supposed to check on the employee situation."

He had forgotten. After thinking about Liz and Kyle, Tess, Isabel being trapped, the blue water, and all those green people, his brain was having trouble considering anything else.

"Well?" he asked.

Maria settled into her chair and grinned. "The regular graveyard shift is supposed to arrive at the hospital at eleven. They'll be let in, but I don't think they're going to let the previous shift go home."

"I'll bet that makes for some tired hospital workers," Alex said.

"Pissed-off ones is my bet," Michael said.

Max nodded. He would have to agree with that.

"What that means," Maria said loudly so that everyone would listen to her, "is that we might be able to get in, but I'm not sure when we can get out."

"That's a chance we're going to have to take," Max said.

"Well, the longer we take at this, the less chance we're going to get to everyone in time." Liz was fidgeting in her chair. She was clearly ready to get moving.

So was Max. He turned to Michael. "I need you to take Alex and Kyle and get that water truck, get it filled and the water treated, and get it dumped into the cave. Do a second load if you don't run into problems, but one load is critical."

Michael nodded and then glanced at Alex and Kyle, who looked less excited about following Michael's lead.

Max did the same. "You both up for helping?"

"Remember that blue water coming out of your tap?" Michael said.

"I said I was in." Kyle frowned as if he'd been insulted. "I haven't changed my mind."

"And I'm not going to miss all the excitement," Alex said. "Although if Isabel needs help . . ."

He didn't finish the sentence. Max understood his predicament, but it was probably better to keep Alex away from Isabel. After all, Alex didn't need the extra ego-blow of meeting Isabel's college-aged date.

Sheriff Valenti tossed Kyle two keys. "That's to the maintenance shed. No point in breaking in if you don't have to. The keys to the water truck are in a small safe. The second key opens it."

"Thanks," Max said to Valenti.

Valenti only shrugged. "Giving them my permission to use the truck keeps them from breaking too many laws."

"Yeah, right," Michael said, smiling at the sheriff.

Max turned to Michael and Alex and Kyle. "You need to get that truck back and the shed locked as quickly as you can."

"No kidding," Michael said, standing. "We'll take care of it, I promise. Two loads if we can, one for sure."

"Try not to be seen," Valenti said. "I don't think anyone will be on the roads tonight, but you just never know."

His unspoken words sent a shiver down Max's back. If the wrong person saw them, they'd never get the cure into the water system.

Max turned to Liz. She looked so serious sitting there, her wide eyes watching him. His heart still jumped whenever their gazes met. He wondered if hers did, too.

"Do you have the stuff they should use to treat the water?" he asked, his voice harsher than usual.

She gave him a small hurt smile, as if she understood the reason for his grumpiness.

"Right here." She picked up some jars from the counter, and handed them to Michael. "Put one jarful in each truckload of water."

"All right," he said, handing one jar to Alex and putting the other in his jacket pocket. "Let's go."

"Not without a kiss for good luck," Maria said, putting her arms around Michael's neck and kissing him hard.

"That should be enough to hold all three of us," Alex said after a few seconds.

Michael finally broke away, tapped Maria on the forehead, and turned away with a "See ya."

"We'll meet back here when we're done," Max said as the three friends headed for the front door of the café.

"Be careful," Maria said.

Max knew he would never get used to sending people, his friends, into danger and trouble. He watched the three of them leave, wishing there was any other way of doing this. There wasn't. Not if he was going to save a lot of people, and keep the attention of the national press and other organizations away from Roswell. And the four alien teens.

Max turned to Liz. "I need you and Maria to try to get into the hospital."

"I'm way ahead of you, Leader Boy," Maria said. "I've already got the uniforms laid out upstairs. I've volunteered at that hospital for years. It won't be a problem."

Liz smiled at Max and he felt the warmth. "I have enough

of the plasma to spike all the water in the place," she said, tapping the pocket on her jacket. "We'll make it work."

Liz handed him three mustard-sized jars. "These are for you three. I've left two other jars this full upstairs in my bedroom, just in case."

"Good," Max said, taking the jars full of his own blood plasma. "Thanks."

Then he turned to Tess and the sheriff. "Looks like it's up to us to break into the army base and see what we can do for the people there."

He handed each of them a jar, then put the one he was keeping in his coat pocket.

"We can do it," Tess said. "We've been in and out of there before."

"I'm counting on that," Max said.

"Let's go get dressed," Maria said, pulling Liz toward the stairs. "We've got to be on time tonight. There are going to be some miracle cures in the Roswell hospital tonight."

"Seems like we specialize in them." Liz gave Max a wide grin.

He didn't smile back. She kept giving him mixed signals and he didn't have the energy for that tonight.

"Max specializes in them," Tess said.

Max felt a surge of irritation. "We wouldn't have solved this without Liz," he reminded her.

"I know," she said and gave Liz a friendly smile. It made him wonder if he had imagined the bite to her previous comment.

Maria continued to pull Liz toward the kitchen door.

"Take care," Max said to them, "and see if you can find Isabel while you're in there."

He wanted to do all of these jobs himself, especially the search for his sister.

"Don't worry," Liz said. "She can take care of herself. You just worry about getting onto that army base and getting those people back to normal."

Max nodded and then with Tess at his side, he turned and headed for the door. Everyone knew what they had to do. Getting it done was going to be another matter altogether.

There was no way Isabel was going to be able to sleep sitting up in a classroom, with a dozen people snoring around her and the lights turned on full. She kept expecting the instructor to come striding onto the stage at any moment and start talking.

Instead the guards remained at their posts, and people either talked in low tones or tried to sleep, or did sleep and snore. The woman ten seats and a row up to her left snored like she was coughing and choking at the same time. She wasn't wearing a wedding ring and Isabel could understand why. No one would be able to get a good night's sleep with her in the room. Maybe after they were released, Isabel would tell the woman to go get checked. She might have some sort of sleep disorder. Her snoring certainly didn't sound healthy.

Behind the woman and six more chairs over, another man, clearly with no difficulty sleeping while sitting up, had a more traditional snore that had some pretty good volume to it and even rumbled the metal on the seats around him. Between him and the woman coughing and choking, it was amazing anyone in the room even dozed.

She eased herself out of the chair and stretched slowly, trying to give her aching muscles and tired mind something to do. Even reading a book would be better than just sitting here, hour after hour.

She moved out of the row and down in front of the stage to where a table full of drinks and rolls were displayed. At least the army was feeding them well so far.

A few men earlier had gotten angry and demanded to talk to someone in charge. They were taken out in the hallway and about ten minutes later came back in with the looks resignation on their faces. Isabel overheard one of them say the doctors were treating this skin problem like a plague and no one was going anywhere any time soon.

Isabel could have told him that.

Over the first few hours after dinner another twenty people had turned green and been taken away. From what Max had told her, it was the alien cells in water that was causing the problem. Those last to turn must have come in contact with the contaminated water later than the ones they had brought in. Or their systems were slower in absorbing it and moving it through their skin systems.

Or, more than likely, they hadn't showered in it, or drunk full glasses of water like the others might have, but instead just touched it somehow. Now Isabel figured there were less than sixty people in the room and the rate of turning green was halted. It looked like everyone in this room who had come in contact with contaminated water had already gone through the change.

Now, things were so quiet she couldn't stop thinking of Rob, and that just got her worrying even more. If only the soldiers would sleep or stop being so vigilant, she might be able to escape. But so far, she hadn't had a single opportunity.

An hour earlier a team of doctors had come in and gone from person to person, asking questions, waking up the snoring ones as well. They had asked Isabel who she had come in with and her relationship to Rob. They seemed satisfied it was only a first date and moved on quickly, which gave Isabel a great sense of relief. The last thing she needed was to be taken and tested for anything.

Behind her the woman coughed and choked, then went right on sleeping. Isabel shook her head, picked up a Danish, and went back to her chair.

It was going to be a very long night. But if the worst that happened was no sleep, she was going to feel lucky about it.

11

Michael could tell he was going to have to use his powers to unlock the fence gate. He motioned for Alex and Kyle to wait in the brush and shadows behind him, and then moved up to the gate and studied the padlock. He wanted to be able to relock the gate again and not have anyone tell that someone had even been here, so he was going to have to open it carefully. Not destroy it in the process.

The county vehicle compound was a fenced yard illuminated by bright, high lights on three poles. It was situated at the end of a road just outside of town off the main highway. A few houses were down the road closer to the highway, but around the yard itself was nothing but brush, some trees, and desert.

The night was getting cold enough that Michael could see his own breath, and his hands were feeling the bite of the spring night as well as he studied the area. There were a dozen different tractors and dump trucks sitting along the fence line near the gate. A large building filled most of the compound, with three large garage doors and a smaller regular door, all facing the gate as well. He had keys from Valenti for the water truck and the building, but not this gate. Maybe Valenti had forgotten it was here, or just didn't have a key to it.

Just to be sure, Michael tried both keys the sheriff had given him on the lock. Neither would even go into the lock hole.

Standing in the light made Michael feel as if he were on a stage and a hundred people were watching. But the Sunday night around him was so quiet, not even a dog was barking. And the few houses that were in sight from the yard had their blinds pulled, more than likely to keep out the light from the compound than a need for privacy.

Michael did a quick check along the fence line to make sure no security cameras were in place, or any alarms, or dogs inside the fence.

Nothing.

Or at least nothing he could see. They would find out soon enough if there was something more. He put his palm over the lock and focused on opening it. After a moment it clicked and fell open, the sound impossibly loud in the still night air.

He pulled the lock free and hung it on the fence, then opened the gate enough to get through and motioned that Alex and Kyle to follow him.

Then he headed at a brisk walk toward the building, Valenti's keys ready in his hand.

Alex and Kyle, moving like thundering elephants, caught him just as he pushed the door open and stepped inside.

"I hate this," Kyle whispered, breathing hard as they looked around the dimly lit garage.

"I'm not loving it," Alex whispered back.

"You volunteered," Michael said.

"You know, I never did stuff like this before I got involved with you guys," Kyle whispered.

Michael bit back a harsh reply. He wasn't real fond of Kyle, either, but Valenti had been a friend more than once. Amazing how a guy with a great dad could turn out so weird.

"Remember green skin," Michael said.

"He's right," Alex said. "There are hundreds stuck like we were. Let's get this done."

"Oh, good, no more whining," Michael said.

"I didn't promise that," Alex said.

The water truck was tucked against the far wall of the garage, on the other side of two dump trucks. On the wall was a huge water tap with a short hose that dropped down into the water truck's tank. A logical setup. Fill the water truck before even taking it out of the garage. Save money, time, and fuel. Seemed almost too logical for the government.

Michael climbed up on the small ladder on the tankers side and shined a small flashlight he had brought into the open tank. "Empty."

"They wouldn't leave it sitting full," Kyle said. "That would rust it out too quickly and be too hard on the tires."

Yeah, Michael understood that, but just once he'd like these things to be easy. The longer they were in the garage, the more likely they'd get caught.

Even Valenti had been worried about that. He'd warned them not to be seen.

Heck, being seen might not be the problem. Being heard might be the problem. Filling the truck wasn't exactly going to be a silent process.

"Swing that hose over here and let's get it started," Michael said.

The hose was larger and heavier than a fire hose and took both Alex and Kyle to boost it up to Michael to put it in the open water truck top.

"I think that's done differently," Alex said after they were finished.

"I forgot to read the manual," Michael said. "Turn on the water. Slowly. I want to make sure all the values on this baby are closed."

Alex twisted the large valve to open up the water flow. The sound seemed to fill the building, echoing and rattling the truck as the water pounded into the bottom of the large tank. Michael was convinced they could hear that much noise all the way to the high school.

"So much for stealth theft," Kyle said.

Michael climbed off the tank and moved around back to the valves that opened to empty the water. They were closed and the truck was filling slowly.

"Turn up the flow," Michael said. "Otherwise this is going to take all night."

Alex moved the water valve to full, and the sound increased to a roar that seemed to shake the entire building.

"Is it supposed to do that?" Kyle almost yelled.

Michael shushed him. The noise from the water was loud enough. Adding shouting to it wasn't going to help.

He moved over to Kyle and put his mouth close to his

ear. "Stand guard at the door, but keep it mostly closed."

Kyle nodded and headed for the door while Michael climbed back up on the truck to see how the water level was. He was stunned to see that the huge tank was almost half full. And rising quickly.

Under him the truck groaned and cracked as the weight was added.

He signaled for Alex to watch him, then as the water got past the three-quarter-full mark, he indicated that Alex should slow the flow down.

Alex did, but the water level was coming up fast.

Michael gave the cut sign, and Alex instantly shut off the water, sending the garage back into a ringing silence.

The truck's shocks creaked a few times as the water rocked and settled in the tank.

Michael again shined his light through the opening. The level was just below the top hatch. Perfect.

Michael pulled out the hose and let it slide down the side of the tanker and bang against the wall. It sounded like a gun-shot and made both Kyle and Alex jump.

"Sorry!" Michael whispered loudly, the sound echoing.

"We're dead," he heard Kyle say, more to himself than anyone else.

"Nothing leaking anywhere?" Michael whispered to Alex.

"Not that I can see or hear," Alex whispered back. "And trust me, in here we'd hear it."

Michael nodded and took out one of the jars of Max's plasma that Liz had given him. He dumped it into the water and then eased the lid of the tank closed, latching it before climbing down.

"All right, let's get ready to open the garage door," Michael said. "Kyle, close and lock that door."

Kyle did as he was told and came to join them. Michael waited, the truck keys in his hand, until they were all together and he could talk softly. "I'll start the truck. Alex, you open the garage door. As he does that, Kyle, you go open the gate."

"We're closing them behind you, right?" Alex asked.

"Absolutely," Michael said. "And lock the gate as well."

Kyle nodded.

"And don't run," Michael said. "From one of the houses down the street we need to look like three workers just taking the truck out for some strange reason on a Sunday night."

Both Alex and Kyle nodded.

"All right, let's do it," Michael said, climbing up into the cab of the truck and settling in. Alex and Kyle moved over to the controls of the garage door and stood waiting.

It took Michael a moment to get situated, find the keys, check to make sure how many gears the thing had. With something hauling this heavy a load of water, it had to have a lot of speeds and he needed to make sure he didn't grind too many gears leaving. The truck was going to make enough noise on its own without him helping matters along.

Finally he was ready. With a deep breath he turned the key.

The truck's engine turned over once and then fired, clearly well-tuned and maintained. The roar was like standing near a jet airport while planes were taking off. Michael had never heard anything like it.

Kyle put his hands over his ears as Alex set the big garage door in front of the water truck in motion. It creaked and squealed so loud, Michael could hear it over the sound of the truck engine. There was no chance they were going to bring this truck back here tonight. They'd leave it out on the road and let them find it in the morning, if the police didn't already have the road barricaded in front of them.

Kyle ducked through the partially open garage door and walked toward the outer gate.

As soon as the door got above Michael's eye level, he eased the shift into low gear and let out the clutch, feeling for the friction point, trying not to jerk the truck and a very heavy load of water forward.

The truck eased toward the door as Alex stepped outside, waiting to close the door behind them.

So far so good. No sign of flashing lights coming for the highway, and the neighbors' blinds were as still as they had been when they got here. Clearly the neighbors were used to people starting up equipment in the middle of the night.

Michael got the truck moving slowly out of the garage and toward the fence gate. As he cleared the door he saw Alex punch the button to lower the door and then jump up on the passenger side running board and open the door.

"So far so good," he said.

Kyle, standing with the open fence gate in his hand looked like he had seen a ghost. They were going to be lucky if he didn't have a heart attack.

Michael got the truck through the gate in low gear and

then stopped, waiting for Kyle to join them.

When he did, Michael looked at him. "Gate locked?"

"Gate locked," Kyle said, his voice squeaking over the sound of the truck.

"Garage door closed?" Michael asked.

"Closed and locked," Alex said.

"Then let's go dump this load," Michael said, easing the truck back forward and not even grinding gears as he double clutched and picked up speed heading for the highway.

Liz stood in front of the guards at the employee entrance to the hospital, the candy-striper uniform feeling odd on her skin. Both she and Maria had worn only light jackets, and the nip in the air was biting at her legs and hands. She hadn't expected to have to wait in a line outside.

In front of them a nurse had just been waved through, and five others were lined up behind them. The graveyard shift was arriving. They had decided that Maria would do all the talking for them, and that was about to happen.

Liz could feel her stomach twist into a knot. She didn't know why. The worst that could happen is that they were turned away and would have to find another method of getting the cure to the people inside the hospital. But so far they hadn't seen an employee sent back to his or her car.

"Name, floor, and job," the guard asked, holding a clipboard in his hand.

Maria, smiling at the man, gave them their names, then told him, "We're going to be doing baby-sitting in the nursery and children's ward. They called us in because the doctors and nurses there were needed on some sort of emergency. Guess that emergency has something to do with you guys being here, huh?"

The guard nodded and searched his list. "I don't see your name on here."

"Of course not," Maria said. "They just called."

"All the additional workers are on my list," the guard said.

Maria rolled her eyes. "They need help in there. I'm sure they're very busy. Do you think they have time to update you every minute?"

He hadn't looked up from his list. Liz shifted from foot to foot trying to stay warm.

"What's the big deal?" Maria asked, putting on her most I-don't-care voice and attitude. "We're just coming to work. Is the emergency that bad that you can't use two extra sets of hands to take care of the kids?"

"Just different," the guard said. "The problem is that unless this is cleared up, you might not be able to leave at your normal time. In fact, there's a good chance you might have to stay tomorrow as well."

Liz shrugged, acting as if she didn't care.

"Stay late, miss school tomorrow?" Maria asked. She held out her arm. "Here, twist it, make me stay longer than usual. Please?"

The soldier actually smiled, then looked at Liz. "Do you care if you're held here longer than expected?"

Liz shook her head. "Not at all. I'd rather be here helping out than taking a math test tomorrow morning. As long as I can call my mom when it gets too late."

The guard nodded. "Not a problem. All right, let me get

your names right and then you can go in to work."

Again Maria repeated their names and he wrote them on his sheet, then they were waved inside as the guard turned his attention to the next hospital employee in line.

"That was too easy," Liz whispered as they headed down the hall.

"Getting in's no problem," Maria said. "But you didn't see anyone leaving, did you?"

Liz knew that was a very good point. As the guard had warned them, getting out was going to take time. But less time if they could get everyone cured.

Maria led Liz down the hall and into the employee lounge. No one was in there at the moment, so they hung their jackets on a coatrack and then Maria led the way through a back hallway to what looked like some sort of small kitchen and service preparation area.

"What are we doing?" Liz whispered as Maria pulled out a water cart. It was in a long line of carts that looked as if they were used on this floor for patients taking pills. They had shelves under the top water cooler area, used more than likely for delivering dinners.

Maria opened up the top of one of the large, silver water containers. "Mostly full. Put a few drops of the cure in each of these, just in case they're used later."

Liz did as Maria instructed, putting just one drop into each cooler as Maria stocked the first cart with lots of paper cups, then went to work on a second.

"Why two?" Liz asked as she finished making sure every water container had the cure in it.

"They're not going to be holding most of the infected people in single rooms," Maria said. "Too many of them, so if we can find where they're holding the main group, we can split up and get them all the cure quicker."

Liz nodded. That made sense. Clearly Maria had given some thought to how to do this once they got inside. Liz had just expected they would play it by ear.

"So where do we go first?" Liz asked.

"Any room that has a guard," Maria said. "We get a few of the green-skinned cured, and the attention will shift to them to see what happened."

"So that no one will pay attention to us helping the larger group?" Liz said. It sounded like a pretty lame plan, but at least it was a plan.

"That's the idea," Maria said, smiling at Liz. "Unless, of course, we find the main group first."

"Okay," Liz said, the knot in her stomach even tighter now.

"Add an extra drop or two in both of these we're using," Maria said. "I want to make sure Max's forces have enough power to do the job."

Liz laughed but did as Maria suggested.

"Ready?" Maria asked.

"As I'll ever be," Liz said.

"Put a smile on the face, and a blank look in those eyes," Maria said. "We're just water girls and know nothing, remember."

Liz tried to smile, but she could tell it came out more like a sick, worried grimace.

"You need acting lessons," Maria said, shaking her head. "Let me do the talking. You just play the dumb follower."

"Play?" Liz said, feeling exactly like a dumb follower.

She'd done her best work. Now it was time to let Maria's outgoing personality shine.

Maria laughed all the way out in to the hallway as she pushed the first cart. Liz followed her with the second cart, doing her best not to bang it into the wall.

12

Max sat beside Tess in Valenti's truck, staring ahead, as the guard looked in the driver's window. Max could feel his stomach twisting as beside him Tess used her powers to make the guard believe that Valenti was taking two generals into the base, not two high school kids.

That was an amazing talent she had. Max wished he knew how she managed it.

He also didn't want to admit how nervous it made him. Sometimes it just seemed too easy. And she accepted it as if it were nothing. At least he knew that his powers were strange.

"Sheriff," the guard said, nodding, "Generals. Go on in."

Then, to Max's surprise, the guard stepped back and saluted.

"Thank you," Valenti said, clearly relieved as the guard finished his salute and the gate opened.

Beside Max, Tess let out a deep breath and slumped a little as Valenti took the truck away from the gate. The base seemed more active than usual. Max had never seen so many trucks driving around the compound.

Just being here made him nervous.

"That was harder than it should have been," Tess said. She sounded drained.

Max felt slightly guilty. He had just mentally accused her of having no real reactions to the use of her powers.

The sheriff shot a worried glance at Tess. He had become almost a father to her, and Max knew that Valenti was feeling protective of her.

"Why was it hard?" Max asked.

"There were three of them," Tess said. "The guard and the two inside watching the monitors. I had to convince them all of the sham."

"Good job," Max said, patting her leg.

She put her hand over his. He wanted to pull away but thought the better of it. He needed everyone's fullest cooperation tonight.

The sheriff turned the truck down a side road in the general direction of where they knew the infected group was being held. No one seemed to notice them, and why would anyone? They were in a truck on an army base, a base filled with vehicles moving back and forth.

"Still," Tess said, "it was harder than it should have been."

Max gave her a concerned look. She had shadows under her eyes that hadn't been there before.

"Well, we're in," Valenti said, parking the truck against a warehouse wall and turning off the lights and engine. The night around them pounded down in silence and almost pitch darkness. This part of the base seemed empty. "Now what?"

Max looked around, trying to get his eyes to adjust to

the change in light. The building in front of them was nothing more than a vague, black shape, with no lights on. Illumination from the front gate area framed another building to the right in silhouette.

"Where, from here, are they being held?" Max asked.

"Three buildings over to the left," Valenti said. "But it's guarded pretty closely."

Max touched Tess again. "Think you can hold the illusion again for a minute?"

"If there's not more than two or three guards," Tess said. "And you and I are going to have to act the part as well."

"Understood," Max said. "Let's get closer and see what we're facing."

The light in the cab blinded him for a moment as they opened the doors and climbed out. Closing the door sounded so loud in the still night that Max was sure it would bring armed guards running. But no one appeared.

They moved to the left, walking down the side of the narrow road as if they belonged there. On a military base, Max had learned it was always best to act as if you belonged. Only guards whose job it was to question everyone stopped you. Everyone else had been so trained to mind their own business that they never bothered anyone who looked like they knew what they were doing, even a sheriff and two high school kids.

At the edge of the third building over Valenti stopped them, and they cautiously looked around the corner of the structure, making sure to stay in the shadows.

"Two guards at the main entrance," Valenti said. "Probably more inside."

"Makes sense," Max said, studying the distance across

the open space between them. The warehouse they were using looked like standard army. Two ambulances, lights off, were parked to one side. Otherwise the guards could have been guarding an empty building as far as anyone was concerned.

"They're not posted to stop people from going in," Tess said, "they're there to stop the infected from getting out."

"So we go in as generals," Valenti said.

"Too hard," Max said, giving one more look at the front entrance to where the infected were being held. He was coming up with a vague plan that just might get them inside and out of sight. He turned to Tess. "Would it be easier to make us look like doctors?"

"Yes," she said. "I don't have to meet as many expectations. I can goof up and they probably won't notice."

"It'll be easier for us to act the part as well," Max said. "That should cover any small mistakes you might make."

She smiled at him, as if she believed he had made that suggestion to help her. He had to admit that hadn't been his first thought. He was mainly concerned about her ability to get them inside the warehouse.

"There are usually second floors on these buildings, aren't there?" Max asked Valenti.

"The ones I've been in have a type of walkway, balcony area," Valenti said. "Usually to post guards and observe experiments."

"That's what I remember as well," Max said. "Stairs are usually through a door to the right of the main entrance."

Valenti nodded. "Yeah."

"We go in as doctors," Max said, "that you, Sheriff, are bringing over from the hospital. We're just there to observe from above."

Valenti nodded. "Sounds good."

Max was glad to have Valenti with him. The man had a real sense of what was possible.

Max turned to Tess. "Can you manage that?"

"I can," she said.

Max took a deep breath. "All right, let's do this."

Striding forward as if they belonged, they headed around the corner and toward the entrance.

"Got them," Tess said softly beside Max.

That meant that she was making the guards ahead believe they were doctors approaching.

"makeup names for us," Max whispered to Valenti without turning his head as they were halfway across the open space toward the entrance. "We're from Albuquerque."

Valenti nodded and didn't break stride.

At the entrance neither guard seemed to be bothered by the three people walking toward them. Again Max figured that was because the concern was holding the infected, not keeping people out.

"I'm Sheriff Valenti," he said as they got close to the guards. "These are Doctors Benning and Stevens from Albuquerque General. They're here to observe."

The guard nodded and actually opened the door for them. "Stairs to the right through the door," the guard said, nodding the door open for them as they went through.

"Thank you, soldier," Valenti said, hardly even slowing down.

Tess and Max both nodded to the soldier holding the

door, but said nothing.

Inside the room smelled like an old warehouse. A door lead straight ahead that was unguarded. Max figured there was at least one guard on the other side of that door to keep the people in.

There was another door to the right. Valenti opened the one on the right to expose a staircase leading up.

When they were halfway up the stairs and the door closed behind them, Tess let out a deep sigh. "Much easier than generals," she said in a whisper.

"Good job," Max said, following closely behind Valenti as they climbed the stairs.

At the top Valenti motioned that they should let him go first since there was no door.

Max and Tess waited, the moldy smell of the warehouse strong now.

"Clear," Valenti whispered.

Max stepped up and walked to a spot where Valenti was standing. It was in the shadows and with the lights so bright below, Max doubted anyone down there would be able to see them.

The sight was amazing, and very overwhelming. At least a hundred cots had been sat up in rows on the concrete floor of the warehouse. Each cot had a green-skinned occupant, and three or four people in white lab coats were moving among the cots.

Almost everyone was sleeping, although a few were sitting on the cots, and a few others were reading. The place smelled like a hospital, or like someone had used too much cleaning solution very recently.

Guards were stationed around the room every twenty

feet or so, rifles in hand. And all the doors into the big space had guards on either side of them.

"How are we going to get the cure to all of them?" Tess whispered.

"Not a clue," Max said, staring at the sight in front of him. It didn't look as if there was any way to get to all those people.

"We're not getting down there, that's for sure," Valenti said.

Max had to agree. Yet somehow, they had to get down there to give the people the cure. Get down there and get out without getting caught.

Impossible was the only word that kept coming to his mind.

Liz was amazed at how many military guards there were at different places in the hospital. It seemed as if every hall-way had at least two, and each of them carried a rifle. And others stood in front of doors, facing inward. The sight of the armed guards in the clean hospital corridors twisted her stomach even tighter. If she and Maria managed to get away with this, she was going to be a mess for days.

Maria, whistling and smiling like there wasn't a care or problem in the world, passed the first guard with a "Hi, soldier!"

The guy didn't respond with anything but a shake of the head.

Liz went by him without a word, gaze locked on her cart. All the doors off the hallway were open, and the first rooms beyond the guard, and across from the guard, contained green-skinned patients. Liz figured that any green-skinned person in a private room had to have either come in first, or was one of the ones the doctors were doing extensive tests on.

Maria stopped her cart, filled a cup full of water, and walked into the room as if she knew exactly what she was doing. Liz pushed her cart to a position past Maria's, near the door across the hall, filled a cup of water and went into that room.

All the time the gaze of the guard seemed to bore into her. She kept her eyes on what she was doing and never looked at him.

The female patient in the room was asleep. She looked to be about seventy, and very frail. The green skin didn't help her appearance at all. Her breathing was labored, and she was hooked up to a heart monitor that was beeping softly.

Liz felt bad about waking her, so she moved toward the bed and then pretended to trip a little. A few drops of the water landed on the woman's green arm.

That should do it.

The woman didn't stir.

Liz sat the cup down on the woman's tray and left.

Maria was already out of her first room and was pushing her cart down the hallway toward the next room.

Liz, again ignoring the soldier standing against the wall with the rifle, did the same, filling another cup with water and moving into the next room.

The person in this room was a man, about her dad's age, who was awake and reading. His skin was a very deep green, and his hair brown with silver tinges.

"Water, sir," Liz said.

"I'm not thirsty," the man said, not even bothering to look up.

"Oh, the doctor said you need to drink this," Liz said.

"At least a sip so I can go to the next room."

The guy, clearly not pleased, took the small cup of water, downed it, and then wadded up the cup and tossed it at the garbage can.

"Thank you, sir," Liz said.

He didn't say a word, just went back to reading.

Liz had no doubt as she turned with a smile that he would be much happier in a few minutes.

They managed to get to every room on the hallway, and were wondering where to go next when a nurse wearing a hat came around the corner.

"Water?" she said. "Good, they need some in the class-room. They're almost out."

She pointed down the hall and went on past, clearly very busy.

Behind them, in the room of the man reading, a shout echoed down the hallway. "Nurse! Doctor!"

Maria grinned at Liz. "Seems a glass of water a day does more than advertised."

"Let's get to that classroom," Liz said, heading her cart in the direction the nurse had pointed. This hallway was mostly offices, their doors closed and the lights off. Two guards stood in front of a set of double doors.

"We were told to bring water to the classroom," Maria said to a young soldier with blond hair and bright blue eyes.

"In here," the guard said, moving aside and opening the door for them. "It goes down in front."

"Thanks, cutie," Maria said, smiling at the young man.

This soldier smiled back at her and at Liz, watching them push their carts through the door before he shut it behind them.

Inside Liz was stunned to see about fifty people, all normal skin colored, mostly sleeping in the seats of the large classroom. Water and other food had been sat up for them on the front stage. A number of people were snoring loudly, the sound echoing around the room.

"This is where Isabel is," Maria whispered so that the guard standing against the wall didn't hear.

Liz scanned the people as they pushed their carts around the outside of the chairs and down a ramp toward the stage. She didn't see Isabel until she and Maria were almost to the front.

Isabel saw them at almost the same time. Her face lit up with surprise and she stood, pretending to stretch.

Then she casually moved out of the row she was in and down toward the front where the water and food was.

Liz glanced around as Maria put her cart in a position where anyone could get a drink from it. None of the guards seemed to be paying anyone any attention. Most of them looked like they were almost asleep on their feet.

"Sure is great seeing you two," Isabel whispered as he picked up a roll. "What are you doing here?"

"We're distributing a cure," Maria whispered, patting the container of water on her cart.

"Does it work?" Isabel asked, clearly stunned.

"Like a charm," Maria whispered. "Green to normal in less than five minutes. We used Max's plasma."

"Amazing," Isabel said softly, shaking her head as she pretended to pick over some of the Danish rolls. "How did you two get in here?"

"In is easy," Liz said.

"Yeah, getting out is another matter," Maria said. "But if we get this stuff to everyone, they won't have a reason to hold us."

Isabel nodded. "I wish I could help."

"You can," Liz whispered. "Make sure everyone in this room has either taken a drink of this water, or has some splashed on exposed skin, just in case they've been contaminated but haven't turned yet. Either method works."

Isabel glanced out over the mostly sleeping people and nodded. "That's going to be difficult, but I think I can manage it given a little time."

"I don't think time is going to be an issue," Liz whispered. "At least not with these people. The ones who are already green are another matter."

Isabel turned and looked right at her. "You telling me the green can become permanent?"

"If we don't get this in or on them in time," Maria said. Liz only nodded.

"And if anyone starts to turn green before you get to them," Maria said, "get some of the water splashed on them before they are taken out. It only takes a drop or so."

"Will do," Isabel whispered. "Good luck." With that she took a Danish roll from the table, a glass of water from Maria's cart, and headed back to her seat.

Liz, with Maria leading the way, pushed her cart back up the ramp toward the doors they had come in. They had a lot of people to find yet. It was going to be a long night, if they didn't get caught.

And even longer if they did.

13

Michael made his way carefully back through the edge of the forest toward where he had parked the water truck, trying not to make any more noise in the brush than he had to. Luckily the night was fairly dark and gave him good cover. After what he had seen near the cave, they were going to need all the help they could get.

The air smelled of pine and fresh pitch, almost as if someone had been cutting trees. There was also a loamy odor that made him think of the fall. That made sense, he supposed. There were probably leaves on the ground, which had been decaying the last few months. No one cleared them here like they did in town.

On the way up the highway, Kyle had thought he had seen some lights in the trees near where the cave was, so Michael had decided it was better to check it out first. He had stayed on the highway and driven past the turnoff they needed to a spot a few hundred yards down the highway and just over a slight rise. There he had backed the truck down onto a short side road and shut it off, telling

Kyle and Alex to wait for him.

They had been awfully quiet on the drive. The human whining had stopped, but he could still feel their nervousness. The next time Maxwell wanted Kyle and Alex to come along on some kind of mission, *he* could baby-sit them.

Michael was beginning to think they were more trouble than they were worth. And he wasn't sure what he was going to tell them about the forest.

What he had found there had surprised him. Scouring the area near the cave were at least fifty army men, many with rifles, most with flashlights. Clearly someone, somewhere, had put together a link between the people turning green in a small area of town and the ground water used by those people in their homes.

So now they were searching the area, and from the looks of the three tents already set up about two hundred yards from the hidden cave, they were going to be there a while.

More than likely they were looking for some physical feature that would have contaminated the ground water, or some chemical spill. There was no way they were going to let three high school students in a stolen water truck dump a load of water into that cave.

He had moved around the searching men, scouting out the entire area, taking his time, trying to come up with some plan that would work. Ideally he'd go back and talk with Max, and together they'd figure out a way to get this done. But Max was somewhere inside the army's base, right about now, if they were lucky. That left Michael to do the planning.

After looking over everything, he thought he had an idea that might work.

The truck loomed out of the darkness ahead of him and he yanked open the door and climbed in.

"Yow!" Alex said, holding his chest, "You scared the crap out of me."

Kyle just looked white. "Warn us next time. What took you so long?"

Yep. Max definitely gets baby-sitting duties next time.

"We got bigger problems than you being scared," Michael said, turning to face the other two in the dark cab. "The army has about fifty men in there scouring the forest."

"Oh, great," Kyle said. "They're going to think we're behind this."

Michael ignored him.

"They figured out the water was contaminated," Alex said softly.

"It sure looks that way," Michael said.

"So much for this idea," Kyle said. He sounded almost relieved.

"No," Michael said. "I think we can still do it."

"You're kidding, right?" Alex asked. "We're not going to drive a stolen truck into the middle of them and just dump the water. They won't believe it's a high school science experiment."

"No," Kyle said. "They're going to think we caused this."

That was the second time he'd said that. Michael couldn't hold back his surge of irritation. "Then they'd be giving us a lot of credit, wouldn't they? The world's most brilliant high school kids."

"Certainly the strangest," Kyle muttered.

Alex put a hand on Michael's arm, probably to calm him. Amazingly, it worked.

"Look," Michael said. "We're going to finish this or these people will be permanently green. Kyle, you think you can drive this thing?"

"I've driven bigger," Kyle said. "But I don't like the idea of driving it into the middle of an army camp. This beast is stolen, you know."

"Actually, technically, your dad let us borrow it," Alex said.

"Yeah, right," Kyle said.

"I want you to drive the truck into the cave," Michael said, handing him the keys, "and I want Alex to empty the water."

"What are you going to be doing?" Alex asked.

"I'm going to be setting up a diversion on the other side of their location that will draw them all away from the cave before you go in," Michael said.

"Are you sure all of them will go?" Kyle asked.

"Oh, trust me, they won't ignore what I'm going to do." Michael didn't tell them he really hadn't figured out exactly what he was going to do, but he figured he could make enough noise to make sure no one either heard or saw the truck.

"Make it big and loud," Alex said.

"It will be," Michael said. "How fast do you think you can get the truck in there and get the load dumped?"

"One minute to get in and backed up to the mouth of the cave," Kyle said.

"Less than a minute to dump the load," Alex said. "If Kyle will climb up on top and open the hatch there when he stops the truck."

"I can do that," Kyle said, nodding.

"Good, it will speed up the flow," Alex said.

"Another half minute back to the highway and out of sight after we dump the water," Kyle said.

Michael nodded. Around him the darkness and silence seemed very deep and heavy. It was the only chance they had of getting this done, as far as he could see. Somehow the cure had to get into the water table, and just dumping it beside the road here wasn't going to do it. The water needed to be dumped down in those rocks in the cave, at the same place the blue cells had gone in.

"Okay," Michael said, "I'm going to create a diversion on the other side of the hill from the cave to get everyone headed over there. One minute after you hear the first explosion, start the truck and come in."

"The *first* explosion?" Kyle asked. "What the heck are you planning?"

"Don't worry it," Michael said. "No one'll get hurt."

Except maybe him. But he didn't add that.

"Where will we meet you?" Alex asked.

"I'm going to double back to the cave," Michael said. "I'll be there before you have to leave. If anyone's around I'll be able to do something to slow them down. You two just move as fast as you can. Understood?"

"And what happens if you're not there?" Alex asked.

"Leave me, take the truck back and park it outside the fence, and head back to the Crashdown."

"You sure?" Kyle asked.

"I am," Michael said, making his voice sound more confident than he really felt. He didn't want to think about the chance he might be left out in these woods with the army looking for him.

"One minute after we hear the first explosion," Alex said. "Got it."

"See you at the cave," Michael said. He opened the door and squinted against the sudden bright dome light, then jumped to the ground, closing the door behind him.

This time, instead of heading into the brush, he started off down the highway at a steady jog. He needed to get around to the other side of the searchers, and the pavement was the easiest and quickest way.

It seemed to take him a long time to get to a position beside the soldiers' locations. They were slowly working their way up the slight hill and had almost reached the top. The cave was now a good three hundred yards behind them, in the opposite direction. More than likely they had already checked it, found nothing, and had moved on.

Michael, being careful to not make any noise, and using the faint illumination from the soldiers' lights, moved down the hill, looking for anything that might work as a diversion. Then up ahead he saw a small building, mostly covered in brush and weeds. It was clear it hadn't been used in years and years.

He crept up toward it and then circled it as best he could, making sure no one was inside. The windows were all broken out on the two walls he could see, and the roof had collapsed. When he got around back, it was clear there was no place inside of this building for anyone to be in. It was mostly just two walls of an old, small shed, held up by the brush and trees that had grown up through it.

Around it were four pretty good-sized trees that towered far out of sight in the darkness above him. This would be perfect. And far enough over the hill that with the attention focused here, they wouldn't see the truck on the other side.

He moved back, working his way through the brush, trying not to swear every time a sharp branch or stick sliced at him. He just wasn't made for this forest stuff, especially at night.

He got about fifty paces away and found a hiding spot behind three large trees. From here he figured he could set off the explosions and make a run for the road. If anyone saw him, they would think he was trying to get to the highway. Then he'd circle back to the cave.

He wasn't planning on anyone seeing him, though.

The line of searching soldiers with their flashlights had just reached the top of the hill and started down. They were spread out about five paces apart, and were moving slowly, searching every inch of the ground around them as they went. Boy, were they about to be surprised.

Michael took a deep breath and reached down inside to the energy he contained within him. Sticking out his hand at the remains of the old shed, he focused on the building and the trees around it, holding the energy back as much as he could until it was a force strong enough to cause a large explosion.

Then he let it go.

The remaining two walls of the old shed exploded in a sound that echoed through the still night, sending sparks and fireballs flashing through the trees, lighting up the entire place brighter than daylight.

Up the hill Michael could see every soldier drop to the ground, guns at ready. They were trained to react, and react they did.

He focused on the large tree stump right beside the now brightly burning shed.

The tree exploded with a second thundering sound, then crashed to the ground up the hill, sending more sparks and shaking everything.

Michael eased back, crawling on hands and knees in the now brightly lit forest until he reached another tree thirty feet farther from the explosions he had just set off. Up the hill some of the soldiers were back on their feet, working their way down the hill, guns ready.

Michael, lying on his stomach, dug up more energy, feeling the drain to his system as he aimed at the tree beyond the cabin.

The huge trunk of that tree exploded, sending wood and bark and fire everywhere.

Again the soldiers hit the ground. Behind them a dozen others came running over the hill. Good, those were the ones that were down in the camp closer to the cave.

Michael again crawled away, moving as fast as he could toward the highway. But he needed to do one more thing to keep them focused. One more explosion.

He crawled around behind a tree and stood, using the tree to block him from the line of sight of the soldiers up the hill. He focused through the smoke and fire around the old shack on a large tree a good hundred paces in the opposite direction he was going to go. Then, closing his eyes, he dug up as much energy as he could, opened his eyes, focused the energy through his hand, and aimed at the tree.

The trunk exploded with the sound larger and louder than anything Michael had heard on the Fourth of July.

Ducking, he ran in the opposite direction, toward the road, as the fire from the last explosion flew through the air. If this had been summer he would have been taking the chance of burning down the entire forest. But luckily, everything was so wet and green from the winter, no fire would spread fast. But he hoped it kept going long enough.

The monster tree whose trunk he had blown up smashed to the ground, shaking everything.

Michael ducked through some brush and out of sight of any of the soldiers. In twenty more paces he was to the highway and running down the road toward where Kyle should have taken the water truck into the forest to the cave. It seemed like a long time had gone by, but he knew it couldn't have been more than two minutes.

That meant if their schedule was right, he still had a minute to get to the cave.

Beside the highway, the forest was lit up like a patio party, the orange flames flickering and illuminating everything.

Michael grinned. When he created a diversion, he created a diversion.

14

Max kept staring at all the people with green skin filling the large warehouse space below him. When they started the day, none of these people had ever thought they would end up spending the night on an army cot, in a cold warehouse, under basic arrest just because their skin was a different color. Those sorts of things just didn't happen any more in this county.

But here it was happening to hundreds, all because no one understood what was causing the skin color change. Or if it was contagious.

Max pulled his jacket tighter across his chest. This place was going to get very cold before the night was out. The army was going to have to bring in heaters pretty soon, or the people down there on that concrete floor were going to be suffering from a lot more than a skin problem.

"I think making you a doctor is our only hope," Tess said. "I can try to hold the illusion with as many as I can while you go down with the cure."

Max shook his head, not looking at her or the sheriff.

"That's just not going to work. There are just too many people."

"If she's willing to try, I say let's go for it," Valenti said.

Max shook his head. He didn't like the fact that Valenti saw no other option. The sheriff usually had some good ideas of his own.

Tess would help, but she never came up with a real plan. As usual, it all fell to Max.

And he had to come up with something.

Around them the balcony was silent. He could feel the tension from the other two caused by his firm answer.

"Sorry," he said, "there's just got to be another way. We just haven't found it yet. If we have to try that idea, we'll do it later, when more people are asleep."

Both Tess and Valenti nodded.

Max forced himself to look up from the floor full of people and study the walls and roof. The warehouse was made of wood and needed to be painted, since the last coat of army green had long ago faded. High windows around the balcony area lit the warehouse during the day, but they were so dirty it was amazing any light got through them. Large light fixtures hung down over the open space like floating ships. Too bad those big lights also didn't let off enough heat to warm this place.

Like focusing a camera, Max suddenly paid attention to the pipes running along the wooden ceiling.

A fire sprinkler system.

He studied it, following one pipe after another. From what he could tell it covered the entire area of the building, and the balcony, and more than likely the front area, with sprinklers spaced every fifteen or twenty feet. They extended down from the ceiling about a half a foot like small red starbursts.

He pointed upward and nudged the sheriff. "What kind of water supply would feed those sprinklers in a place like this?"

Valenti followed where he was pointing. "Depends. I've seen older ones with water supplies on the roofs, others run off of city water with supply tanks only as backup. It would depend on the water supply to these warehouses, I guess."

"Perfect," Tess said, staring at the sprinklers over them. "Simple and perfect."

"Maybe," Max said. "We have to solve two problems first. One is the water supply. Can we get to it?"

Valenti frowned. Tess peered into the darkness as if she could find the answers without moving.

Max turned and headed back for the door to the stairs. He didn't remember seeing any more stairs leading upward in the stairwell, but he bet that's where they would be.

Valenti followed him. Tess remained by the rail. Max was irritated that she didn't seem to be trying to help, until he remembered how much effort she had used, convincing the guards that the two of them were doctors.

He wondered if his feelings about Tess would ever stop being mixed.

When he reached the door, he stopped. His theory was close to being right. There was a ladder on the wall beside the stair doorway. The ladder led up to a closed trapdoor in the roof twenty feet above the balcony.

"I don't know if we can climb up there without being seen," Valenti said, giving voice the very fear that Max had.

"Sheriff, you and I have to try." Max turned. Tess kept looking at them over her shoulder.

He went to her side. "Tess, you keep an eye on anyone below who happens to look up this way. Try to block what they are seeing if you can."

"I can do that," she said. She moved over to a spot where she could see the floor below fairly well and then nodded to Max to go ahead.

Max went back to the door. He wondered if the people below could hear him moving around. He hoped not.

The sheriff started to go first, but Max stopped him. "If that's locked up there, I need to be in front to open it."

Valenti nodded. "I'll wait until you're on the roof."

"Good," Max said, then moving as smoothly and silently as he could, he climbed the wooden ladder. His fear had been right. There was a padlock at the top of the ladder and it took him a moment to unlock it, holding on to the ladder with one hand while grabbing the lock with the other. He was very high above the ground. Not that he was afraid of heights, but hanging with one hand on an old wooden ladder wasn't his idea of a fun Sunday evening.

He got the lock loose and pushed the trapdoor open, then climbed up onto the roof.

Down below, Tess glanced up and nodded, then went back to focusing on making sure anyone below who looked up wasn't going to see the sheriff climbing the ladder.

Max held the trapdoor barely open until Valenti got near it, pulled it all the way back so the sheriff could climb through, then closed it behind him.

The roof was dark and even colder than inside. A slight

wind was blowing from the west, and the lights of Roswell lit the sky to the south. It was a nice night, but not one Max had time to enjoy.

The roof was made of black tar, and the shapes of the fans, pipes, and other stuff sticking out made Max feel as if he'd walked into horror funland at a carnival. The shadows were everywhere and seemed to move in the wind, even though Max knew that was his imagination.

"Where would the water tank be?"

"If there is one," Valenti said, "my guess it would be covered and in a building protection of some sort. Walk lightly, our footsteps might echo in the warehouse below."

Max nodded, feeling like he needed to whisper as well as tiptoe.

Valenti pointed to a shape looming off the roof on the other side, a faint shape against the lights of Roswell beyond. They started toward it, moving carefully. The closer they got, the more the shape looked like a small building stuck on the flat roof like an afterthought.

"I bet that's the utility area," Valenti said. "A water tank would be in there, and the electrical access, and the plumbing from the city water."

Another padlock was on the room's door, but Max opened it quickly.

A black room greeted them, the door seemingly an entrance into nothingness. There just wasn't enough surrounding light to illuminate the inside.

Valenti stepped into the darkness, and Max waited, standing to one side of the door to give him what little light he could.

"There's a switch here by the door," Valenti said. "Come

in and close the door so I can turn it on."

Max stepped inside and closed the door, plunging them into pitch blackness. There wasn't even a speck of light coming in under the door. Good, light from the inside wouldn't show up to someone happening to look up this way.

A moment later Valenti turned on the light, shocking Max with the brightness of one bare bulb.

"There," Valenti said, pointing to a large tank that filled most of the left side of the room.

They both moved over and studied the rusted metal tank. It was about ten feet tall and as wide around as a house. A valve on one side of it with a large handle said WATER CUTOFF.

"This tank feeds the automatic sprinkler system," Valenti said, pointing at the big thing, "and is refilled by this pipe here from the base's water supply."

"So is there enough water in that tank to get everyone below wet?" Max asked.

Valenti laughed. "More than enough. You set that off, and they're going to think they're in a spring cloudburst."

"Just from that tank?" Max asked.

"Just from the water in the tank, if it's full," Valenti said.

"Then we need to shut off the water supply to it," Max said. "No point in diluting the cure once it's on the people."

"Good point," Valenti said.

Max looked around at the electrical panels and other pipes. "Think we can trigger the system from here?"

"No," Valenti said, "we're going to need some heat on the sensors down below I'm afraid."

Max had figured that would be the case. He could set

off the sensors, heat them up enough to trigger the water, but it was going to be risky doing so with army guards all around.

"Okay," Max said, moving over to the center of the big tank, "boost me up on top so I can put some of the plasma in the water."

Max couldn't bring himself to call it his own blood. He was thinking of it as a cure, not that he was bathing people in his blood cells.

Valenti locked his fingers together and boosted Max up on the tank, banging one toe as he did on the side of the tank, sending a bell-like sound through the room.

Max froze, holding his breath until the sound faded.

"Wonder what that sounded like down below?" Valenti whispered.

Max didn't want to think about that. Carefully he moved to the center of the tank where there was a hatch, more than likely used to let workers down inside to clean the thing. He opened the hatch and looked down at the black surface of the water.

"It's full," he whispered.

"Good," Valenti said. "I'm turning off the base water refill."

Max opened up one of the small jars that Liz had given him and dumped it in. It didn't seem like much in that huge volume of water.

He studied it for a moment, then took out another jar and emptied it as well. He might as well make sure there were enough of his plasma cells in the water to make the cure work. That left one in his pocket for anything else that might come up. This was the only chance they had to help these people.

He closed and secured the hatch on the tank, then, with Valenti's help, crawled down without making any more loud sounds.

Three minutes later they were back beside Tess on the balcony.

"Any problems?" Max asked as he knelt beside her and looked at the green people below.

"A couple guards looked up here and saw only shadows," Tess said. "And your little bell-ringing made a few look at the ceiling, but nothing else. How about you?"

"Treatment in the sprinkle water supply," Max said.

"We're ready to go," Valenti said.

"Let's get back by the stairwell door," Max said. "Tess, be ready to put disguises on us with anyone we meet."

"I'm always ready," she said. "I want to get out of here alive, remember?"

Max nodded, then focused his energy on the sprinkler head right over the middle of the warehouse. He imagined it getting hotter and hotter, flames licking at it.

Suddenly it let go with a popping sound, and water flowed from it down on the people below.

Before anyone could even shout, more of the sprinkler heads popped, and the alarms went off. But not all of the floor was being covered with water yet.

"They're in sections," Valenti said. "You're going to have to trigger each section."

Max focused on another area, heating the heat sensor until that area of sprinklers let go.

Then he did it on the next.

And then finally on the last.

When he stopped, all the sprinklers over the warehouse were soaking everything below them with very special water. Alarms were ringing, people were shouting.

And every guard at every door was looking very intense, guns at the ready as the water poured down on the green-skinned people unable to find shelter.

"Those poor people are in for a cold and wet night," Valenti said. "The guards aren't letting them get to shelter."

"But they're going to be happy anyway," Max said, noticing that on some of the wettest people, the green was almost gone, as if it was simply being washed off.

Down below a few started to notice the change, standing in the shower of water, welcoming it.

Doctors ran out of a side door and into the water, just as the downpour slowed and then dropped to a trickle. Even over the fire alarms, Max could hear the laughing and shouting for joy as the green seemed to just vanish from everyone's skin.

"That's some strong stuff you put in that water," Tess said, smiling at Max.

"Decided to give it a double dose just to make sure," Max said. "No point in taking any chances."

"So while all the fun is happening," Valenti said, "any ideas about how we try to get out of here?"

Max shook his head, looking at the craziness on the warehouse floor below. "Too many people moving too fast for Tess to control their thoughts. Let's just move around to a place on the balcony, out of the way, and away from the door, and wait until things calm down."

Valenti nodded, smiling. "Sounds like a good plan to me. After all the climbing on the roof, I could use a rest."

Max led the way, catching glimpses of the very happy and very wet people below them. He really wanted them all to calm down quickly, and maybe be moved to dry quarters. He was worried about Liz and Maria and Isabel and all the people with green skin in the hospital. He felt he and Tess and Sheriff Valenti needed to get there, but right now, it was just too dangerous even to try.

If there was one thing he was staring to learn, sitting and waiting was sometimes the best thing he could do. And this was one of those times.

15

Michael ran up the dirt road toward the cave. The night was lit up by the fires he had started on the other side of the shallow ridge, and he could see the water truck backed up to the cave, as well as the army tents and a dozen army trucks and jeeps just up the hill. A line of soldiers were standing on the top of the ridge, staring over at the fires on the other side, not paying any attention to the water truck behind them.

At least his diversion was working so far.

The air smelled of smoke and ash, and burning tree sap. He could hear the flames crackle, even from this distance. His lungs were burning.

He was less than a hundred paces from the truck when Alex finished dumping the water in the cave and scrambled for the passenger door. From the looks of it, their mission had been accomplished. The treated water was headed down into the water table.

Now if they could just get out of here alive.

Kyle started the truck in motion toward Michael before

Alex was even in the passenger side.

At that moment a soldier at the top of the ridge turned around and pointed. He might have also been shouting, but in all the noise from the explosions and truck engine, Michael couldn't hear him.

Michael hoped no one else could, either.

Two of the soldiers with guns raised them, pointing them at the water truck.

"Stop!" The shout echoed through the trees.

That one Michael heard.

He didn't much like the soldiers pointing rifles at the truck or him. One stray shot into the old thing's gas tank and they'd all be burning.

Summoning all of the energy he had left, he aimed his explosive power at a tree trunk that was between the men with guns and the water truck. The tree trunk blew up like a bomb had hit it, sending the soldiers on the ridge scrambling for cover behind anything they could find. It would have been comical if it wasn't so serious.

The explosion had been awfully close to them. Michael hoped the soldiers weren't hurt.

Michael motioned to Kyle to keep going and not stop the big truck. It was still moving slow enough that he could get on. As Kyle passed, Michael grabbed on to the passenger side mirror and jumped up on the narrow running board, using the big water tank as shelter from the soldiers.

Bullets ripped into the ground beside the truck.

"They're shooting at us!" Alex shouted.

"They're what?" Kyle shouted, his eyes the size of saucers as he fought the old truck down the dirt road.

Holding on tight with one hand, Michael aimed his power at one of the biggest army trucks. It was the closest one. He figured if those guys were stupid enough to shoot at people who were trying to help, then they were going to pay with a truck or two.

Giving the energy an extra shove, he blew up the big truck.

The explosion shook the air as the army truck lifted into the air, did a perfect half-flip and landed upside down.

A moment later its gas tank exploded, sending it spinning down the hill.

That ought to slow them down some. But just to be sure, Michael managed to get enough energy to bring down a large tree across the road right behind them.

"That won't stop them for long," he said, opening the door and swinging inside as Kyle pounded the truck toward the paved highway.

"Which way?" Kyle shouted, the panic clear in his voice.

"Turn away from town," Michael said. "I know where we can ditch this monster before anyone gives chase."

"And walk back to town?" Alex asked, almost shouting over the loud engine. "Are you kidding?"

"I'm not walking back," Michael said. "But we are going to have to put some distance between us and this truck."

His throat was sore, too. It hurt to talk. There had to be more smoke in the air than he could smell right now.

He glanced behind him. The entire night sky was lit by the fires he'd started. He wondered how the army would ever explain this one.

Knowing them, they probably wouldn't even try.

He took out his cell phone and waved it at Kyle and Alex. "We'll call for a ride when the coast is clear."

"If anyone's back yet," Kyle said, bouncing the truck onto the highway and heading away from the orange light of the fires in the forest, grinding gears as he gained speed.

"Oh, we won't call until morning," Michael said. "Let's hope someone's back by then."

"Great," Alex said. "A night in the cold. I should have dressed for it."

"Better than a night in jail," Michael said, watching the mirror to make sure no one was following.

So far the road was empty. But he knew it wasn't going to stay that way for long.

"Up ahead," Michael said, "turn left off the highway and take the dirt road down toward the stream. Trees and brush will cover this beast from sight from the highway and the air."

"We're not more than a quarter of a mile from the army," Kyle said. "You want to stop *now*?"

"And who would look for us in their back pocket?" Michael asked.

"Besides," Alex said, "we're not going to be able to outrun anyone in this thing."

Michael nodded. He felt relief that Alex was along. When things got really tough, Alex always came through.

So did Kyle, if Michael was being fair about it. Only with Kyle the coming through involved a lot of complaining.

The truck's shocks were shot. It bounced along. Michael felt like his teeth were going to rattle out of his head.

Behind him, he heard more shouts and another explosion. Probably some sap igniting. He was even more relieved now that the weather had been cool and damp.

Even so, it would take the Army a long time to put out these fires. And they'd use a lot of water to do it. Anything that flushed the cure deeper into the water table helped right now.

"There!" Michael pointed to the dirt road and Kyle hit the brakes. He expertly swung the old water tanker off the highway and down the dirt road, bumping them far too fast over rocks and washouts.

"Slow down!" Alex shouted. "I want to live to get out of this cab."

"And then kill the lights," Michael said.

Kyle slowed down enough to make out the road without the lights on, then slowly eased the truck through more ruts and to a place under some trees, sheltered from the road.

When Kyle shut off the engine, the silence seemed almost louder than the noise had. Michael could feel his heart pounding and the exhaustion from using his powers so much. What he needed more than anything was a nap, but he wasn't going to get it anytime soon.

The engine cracked and the tank behind them settled, the sounds seemingly extra loud in the silence covering them. Michael's eyes were starting to adjust to the darkness. He could see the stream in front of them and the grassy meadow beyond.

"Well, I don't want to do that again," Alex said, sighing.

"I can't believe I was even involved," Kyle said. "I feel sick. They were shooting at us back there."

"Am I going to have to pry your fingers off the steering wheel?" Alex asked.

"Maybe," Kyle said, "if my heart ever stops trying to hammer its way out of my chest."

"How did you know about this place?" Alex asked. "It looks nice."

"Maria found it," Michael said. "Ask her how."

The memory of the wonderful afternoon they had spent here last summer flashed in his mind. Now that memory was going to be replaced by this one. Too bad.

"I just might," Alex said with a grin.

"Okay," Michael said, his voice sounding almost too forceful in the darkness. "We have to get moving. Kyle, give me the keys. We have to make sure they get back to your dad."

Kyle took them out of the ignition. "You want me to hold on to them for him?"

"No," Michael said, barely seeing Kyle's face in the dark, "in case we're caught, I don't want you to have them. That's too much of a direct line to your father."

Michael saw Kyle nod in the dim light, then hand the keys over.

"Now we have to wipe down everything we've touched on this truck," Michael said. "And some things we didn't."

"Why do that?" Kyle said. "Our fingerprints aren't on file, are they? Mine aren't."

"No, we need to do it to make it look more like a professional job," Alex said. "Right?"

"Exactly," Michael said. "We want them to think it was someone with prints on file that took this, not high school kids."

"Oh," Kyle said.

"I'll hotwire the ignition," Michael said, "to make them think there were no keys, while you guys are wiping things down. Don't forget the valves in the back and the ladder to climb up on top."

Kyle started to get out.

"Not yet," Michael said. He reached up, covered his fist in his jacket, and smashed the dome light over Alex's head, making sure the bulb was broken as well.

"Again good thinking," Alex said. "But you could have warned me."

"Sorry," Michael said.

"When did you become such a master criminal?" Kyle asked. "You seem to know all the tricks."

"When you grow up like I did, you have to learn to adapt," Michael said. "Let's get to work. I want to be away from this truck as soon as we can."

"Yeah, so do I," Alex said.

"If never see this thing again I'll be happy," Kyle said.

"At least we got the water supply taken care of," Alex said. "No more green people."

"Let's hope," Michael said.

Above them on the highway a police car flashed past, its red-and-blue lights flashing, heading in the direction they had been going. At the speed it was going, it wouldn't have taken long to catch this old truck. By sunrise they were going to have to be a long ways away from here, that was for sure.

And even then they might not be safe.

Liz was stunned at the change in the hospital that had occurred by the time she and Maria got the one cart out of the classroom where Isabel was being held prisoner. Before it had seemed very quiet and somber, now it was buzzing with excitement. Doctors ran down the hallway, and the intercom was calling out names to come to the emergency wing.

"Guess we caused a little stir," Maria whispered, laughing. "Which way?"

"The opposite of the one we came," Liz said. "I don't think we want to be seen on that hallway again."

"Good point," Maria said. She headed off to the right, pushing the water cart ahead of her, looking in every door as they went.

"Do we still need both carts?" Liz asked as they walked along, ignoring the rooms with regular people in them. A glass of water with Max's plasma in it wasn't going to help a cancer patient.

"No, there's enough in here to do the trick." Maria patted the water container on the cart. "We just need to find where they're keeping everyone."

"I'll bet that most of them are going to be in one place," Liz said. "Like Isabel and the rest were being held in that classroom. Any room that big in the hospital that you know of?"

Maria thought for a moment as they stepped aside to let a nurse run past. "Everything on the second floor is maternity and children's wards. The only place I can think of might be the lobby on the third floor. It's sort of a big atrium area with a cafeteria off to one side."

"Would it hold a few hundred people?" Liz asked.

"Sure," Maria said.

"Then third floor it is," Liz said.

"There must be a lot of thirsty people up there," Maria said.

"I'm sure of it," Liz said, smiling.

Liz was glad that Maria was keeping the mood light and the attitude good. It was helping her deal with the fear of getting caught. She didn't know why this bothered her so much, but it sure did, even though they were doing nothing illegal. It was more the fear of someone discovering what they were giving out and tracing it back to Max and the others.

The elevator was empty, and they made it easily to the third floor. When they got off, they faced two men in army uniforms, both carrying rifles.

"Your business here?" one soldier asked, his face frowning at the sight of them.

Liz's stomach went right back into the twisted knot it had been in before they found Isabel.

"What does it look like?" Maria asked, smiling at the guy. "We have the wonderful task of making sure, under doctor's orders, that everyone gets exactly one glass of water. You want to help?"

"No," the soldier said. "Proceed."

"Thanks, cutie," Maria said.

This time the soldier didn't respond, just stared straight ahead, looking past them.

Liz watched as the other soldier managed not to laugh, but Liz wasn't sure how. Clearly the one guy was far, far into playing guard, and the second soldier found it funny.

The second soldier winked at Liz when he saw her smiling. She could feel herself blush. She smiled back at him and moved on with Maria, the knot in her stomach again loosening.

"Flirting at a time like this?" Maria asked, smiling at Liz with a twinkle in her eye.

"Any chance I get," Liz said, laughing.

Around the corner the hallway emptied into a large open area with dark skylights above. A few trees were growing out of some planters in the middle of the space.

It would have been pretty if there weren't so many green-faced people lying and sitting around, all being watched over by stern-faced soldiers.

Maria was still smiling at Liz when they rounded the corner. But when she looked around, she stopped dead cold.

After a moment she turned to Liz, then went back to moving the cart. "Oh, we have a problem," Maria whispered, shoving the cart against one wall and pretending to get supplies off a lower shelf.

"What?" Liz asked.

"This stuff works too fast," Maria whispered. "We won't get through half of these people by the time the excitement starts. And then we'll never get to the others."

Liz looked around at all the people sleeping on cots, sitting on benches, lying on blankets on the floor. There had to be well over a hundred of them, at least.

And half of them were asleep. They'd have to wake them up even to get them to drink, or somehow put drops of water on their skin without anyone noticing.

Maria was completely right. One drink, one person at a time wasn't going to work. Not even close.

"Any ideas?" Maria asked, standing and looking out at the crowd of people.

"Not a one," Liz said.

"I was afraid you'd say that."

They both just stood there, staring at what seemed to be an endless sea of green skin.

16

Michael moved slowly around the old water truck in the dark, whispering to Alex and Kyle, wiping off things himself as he went. He and Alex both had gone over the interior of the truck, wiping down everything from the dashboard to the roof and seats. Now, with one final walk around the truck to make sure they hadn't missed anything, including the mirror he had grabbed on the run, it was time to get away from here.

Around them the night was mostly still, the stars above the trees out clear and cold. At least a dozen police and military vehicles had sped past them in the last fifteen minutes. And in the distance the orange glow from the fires Michael had caused had died down and disappeared. That was good, because the last thing he had wanted to do was start a forest fire.

"Would you look at this?" Alex said, pointing at a spot on the back of the truck right above the valve that opened the water flow. "A bullet hole."

"Not funny," Kyle said.

"A couple feet down and it might have hit the gas tank," Alex said.

"Again not funny," Kyle said.

Michael glanced at where Alex was pointing and nodded. "He's not being funny. That is a bullet hole. Let's get going."

"I can't believe I was shot at by army soldiers," Kyle said, staring at the hole, then turning to follow Michael.

"Believe it," Alex said.

"Just don't tell anyone about it," Michael said as he worked his way carefully down the path toward the small stream, letting his eyes adjust even more to the darkness ahead.

"You think I'm that stupid?" Kyle asked.

"I didn't say that," Michael said. "Just no pillow talk, all right? At least until I'm a long ways from this town. We could get put away for a lot of years for what we did tonight, no matter how good our reasons were."

"Not counting what you did to those trees and truck," Alex said, laughing.

"I don't have a girlfriend at the moment, and if I did, I certainly wouldn't admit to hanging out with you two hoodlums," Kyle said, sounding offended.

"Good," Michael said, leading the way down toward the stream and away from the road.

"Watch your step in the dark," Alex said. "Twisting an ankle now would just about doom us."

"Great," Kyle said. "Where exactly are we heading?"

"I figure we have about seven hours until sunrise," Michael said. "We need to be over on Launder Road by then."

"Launder?" Alex asked. "That has to be at least three miles across open desert."

"No chance," Kyle said. "I've been out on that desert in the daylight. At night it would be almost impossible."

"Do you have another idea?" Michael asked, stopping beside the small stream and turning to face the other two. Behind them the truck seemed like a large, dark shape looming in the night. The air was cold, biting at his nose, and he could see his breath in the starlight.

On the highway a cop sped past, his lights flashing, illuminating the trees around them with bright blues and reds.

"There are going to be roadblocks going both directions," Michael said. "And pretty soon they're going to start searching side roads. They'll find the truck by noon, I can guarantee that."

"We need to be sitting in the Crashdown having breakfast by then," Alex said.

"Exactly," Michael said. "And the only way I can see it happening is if we cut over to Launder Road and call to have someone pick us up."

"Launder Road goes into town a different way than this one does," Alex said. "It won't have the roadblocks. That makes sense now that you mention it."

"Nothing about that desert out there makes sense," Kyle said. "Trust me."

"Just watch your step very carefully," Michael said, "and we'll be fine."

He turned and jumped over the small stream, then headed up the trail on the other side toward the meadow where he and Maria had the picnic last summer. But this time he was going to go around the meadow, through the stand of trees and out into the rocks and brush of the desert beyond.

At best it was going to be a long night.

He didn't want to think about the worst.

The complete celebration and pandemonium of the warehouse had finally died down as aid workers came in with dry clothes, new bedding, and blankets, and doctors checked over everyone they could reach who had once been green-skinned. For a good half an hour the place had been like a circus.

Max had moved Tess and Valenti back into the shadows of the balcony as a half dozen soldiers came up and then climbed the ladder to the roof. Luckily Max had relocked both the door to the water tank and the roof door, so it didn't seem as if anyone had been up there.

After a short time the men came back down, locking the trapdoor as they did, and went down the stairs.

"They don't have any idea what they're looking for, do they?" Valenti asked.

"Nope," Max said, smiling. This had worked better than he had ever hoped it would. There was no doubt the army was going to hold these people for most of the night, but by the time morning came along, and no one was turning green, and there were no symptoms of any disease, they would all be let go. The army had no other choice in the matter. Holding them now would cause a stink that not even the army could live down.

Max just hoped that Maria and Liz were having the same luck at the hospital. If not, this cure here was going to really confuse the issue with everyone there. His little voice kept telling him that he needed to get there to help them, even though he had no idea what was happening.

Finally, after a good fifty aid workers and doctors had come and gone and come back again down below, Max couldn't stand waiting any longer. He turned to Tess. "Are you up for making us appear as doctors again?"

"I think I can do it," Tess said, "if we watch the number of people we're facing."

"Let's go, then," Max said. "We need to get to the hospital and find out what's going on there."

"Worried, huh?" Valenti asked. "So am I."

"That's not what I wanted to hear," Max said.

With Tess leading the way by one step, they went down the stairs to the door at the bottom. As Tess stood nearby, Max eased the door open just a crack to see who was out in the main lobby. Only two soldiers at the moment.

"You ready?" he whispered to Tess.

She nodded, moved to a position where she could see the two soldiers through the crack, then opened the door wide and held it for the sheriff.

"Gentlemen," Valenti said, walking past the two guards as if he knew what he was doing. Tess and Max stayed very close behind him.

Valenti stopped as he opened the outer door. "Doctors," he said.

"Thank you, Sheriff," Max said as he followed Tess out the door.

Outside there were two more guards, and a few people standing a distance away near some cars. Only the two guards glanced their way, nodded, and went back to staring off in the distance.

Tess must have gotten to them quick enough to do the illusion as well. This had to be very difficult for her.

Valenti walked between Tess and Max and the three of them moved at a steady pace across the open area in front of the warehouse to the corner of the next building and out of sight of the guards.

Tess staggered and Valenti caught her, keeping her walking toward his truck.

"Good job," Max said, moving around so that he could be on the other side of Tess and help keep her moving. "Are you going to be all right?"

"Yeah," Tess said, her voice weak and raspy, "I just need to sit down for a minute."

They managed to get her into the truck, and a moment later Valenti had it headed for the gate.

It was clear to Max that Tess wasn't going to be able to hold one or two guard's focus at the gate while they went through. They were going to have to try something else, and fast.

"Let's get down on the floor," he said, scooting down and then pulling Tess after him.

"I can do it," Tess complained but didn't fight as Max helped her get as low as she could.

Valenti headed the truck toward the main exit to the base. Max knew that the guards at the gate seldom stopped outgoing traffic, especially someone like the sheriff who had checked in earlier. Now it would look like he was just leaving without the passengers he brought in.

Or at least that was what Max hoped it would look like.

Max eased down into a lower position and stuffed his body around Tess's. "You need to make sure if someone looks in," he said, talking in her ear, "they see nothing."

"Will do," Tess said, nodding. "Warn me, Sheriff, by clearing your throat."

"Okay," Valenti said. "Stay down, we're almost there."

Max moved his head all the way down and behind Tess, leaving her a clear vision if anyone looked into the truck on the driver's side. He didn't like lying there basically blind, but it was the best way at the moment.

Valenti slowed, then waved and sped up.

"Passed us right through," he said after a moment. "Stay down for another ten seconds until we get far enough away."

"It feels good to be out of that base," Max said, working to help Tess start to climb off the floor and back up on the seat.

"That it does," Valenti said. "Good job in there, both of you."

"Thanks," Max said. "But I have a hunch this night's not over yet."

"I'm headed for the hospital now," Valenti said. "It's clear. Climb on up."

"Easier said than done," Max said as he and Tess struggled to get untangled enough to climb up on the seat of the truck. It felt strange being that close to her again. Almost normal and right.

She sure didn't seem to mind him touching her, that much was clear. And when they finally got back on the seat, she scooted against him and laid her head on his shoulder and closed her eyes.

For the entire distance to the hospital, he enjoyed the feeling of her being comfortable against him. A feeling that he had only had before with Liz.

17

Liz knew after ten minutes of standing there, pretending to be getting the water cart ready, that they weren't going to come up with a way to get to everyone fast enough, no matter how much they thought about it. There just wasn't an answer. There was only two of them, far too many green-skinned people, and not enough time.

Around them the snores of some of the patients filled the large space. A few others paced along the wall, clearly not happy with being either green-skinned, or trapped here. Many just sat and either read or stared off into the distance.

"I say we just go for it," Maria said. "We spill, we shove, we dribble, and we get water on every one of them as fast as we can. Half of them are asleep, so we don't even wake them, just walk by them dripping."

Liz stared at the soldiers around the large hospital atrium. "And we do this without being seen?"

"Of course not," Maria said. "We try not to get seen, but if we're fast enough, by the time anyone realizes it's the water, we're downstairs hiding."

Liz again looked at all the green people. A few doctors had come up, checked a few patients, and then gone back down the elevator. Clearly the sudden cure of those green-skinned people in that one wing had everyone excited, and focused down there, not up here.

"Okay," Liz said. "Let's do it. Remember, one drop on them is all we need. So don't drench anyone."

Maria smiled. "Not unless I have to."

"Great," Liz said, shaking her head. Her stomach was twisting so hard now, she could hardly take a breath. Yet somehow she had to smile, be polite, and move fast.

"You start down the far side, I'll go this way," Maria said, handing Liz a tray full of cups of water. Even though the small, paper cups were only half full, the tray was surprisingly heavy.

Liz took a deep breath. "I figure we have about ten minutes before the first signs really become clear, maybe less. Keep going if we're close."

"I know," Maria said. She smiled at Liz. "On your mark . . ."

"Get set . . ." Liz said back.

"Go!" the both said at the same time.

Liz turned and headed for the far side of the room, dipping her hand in one of the glasses to make sure there were drops on her fingers. As she passed the first sleeping man who was snoring in coughs and spurts, she dripped a few drops on his arm, then moved to the next man, doing the same, pretending to see if he was awake.

The third person along the far wall was a woman, reading a novel.

"Water," Liz said, holding the cup out for the woman to take. "You need to drink it quickly."

"Why?" she asked, not even glancing up at Liz as she reached for the cup.

Liz hesitated just long enough that while letting the cup go it sloshed a few drops on the woman's green hand. "Doctor's orders," Liz said, moving on.

She managed to drip some water on three more sleeping people without being seen by any of the guards, sloshed two more cups of water on two more people clearly not interested in drinking, and then turned back down the second row.

Across the room Maria was making about the same progress.

It seemed as if it was going slowly. Far too slowly. They weren't going to make it to everyone. Maybe not even the center two aisles of people, depending on how much of a ruckus the first people made when they saw themselves turning color.

Liz felt her heart was racing so fast it would explode out of her chest. And the knot in her stomach had become so hard, she doubted she was ever going to be able to eat again.

She followed the same routine along the second row of green patients, handing glasses to the ones who were awake, sloshing on many, dripping water on the sleeping ones as she passed. If she was being graded on her performance as a helper, she was failing.

But so far she had made sure everyone she passed had either drank some of the water, or had the water dripped on their skin.

She was all the way to the end of the second row when the woman who had been reading the novel stood, moved over, and faced her. She was a good foot taller than Liz, about ten years older, and was clearly very smart. She was smiling at Liz, her blue eyes almost laughing as she blocked Liz's way.

"Yes?" Liz asked, not sure what to do or say to the woman who was facing her.

"I've been watching you and your friend since you spilled that water on me," she said, too soft for the guard standing ten feet away to hear. She held out her hand she had been covering. It was back to its normal flesh color.

"I don't know what you are doing," the woman said, "and I don't care why you're not telling the doctors about it, to be honest. As long as it works and gets me out of here."

"It works," Liz whispered. "You'll be back to normal skin color in about five more minutes. No side affects and no chance of the green skin coming back."

"Okay, then," the woman said, nodding. "You're going to need some help getting this done. Is that water over there in that container the same stuff you're using?" The woman pointed to the cart.

"It is," Liz said, stunned that the woman was offering to help with the cure.

"Keep going, then," the woman said.

She headed for the cart. Liz watched her for a second, then glanced at Maria, who had this horrified look on her face.

Liz gave her a thumbs-up and went back to dripping water on the sleeping green people.

The woman took a tray, filled about ten paper cups, and started down the center row between Liz and Maria, the row Liz was convinced they would never reach.

It was clear to Liz, and anyone who looked, that the woman's arm was normal color, as well as half her face. But none of the guards seemed to be noticing. A couple of the awake patients did, but she whispered something to them, and they took a cup and drank it without a word.

One of them, a man in his middle thirties, even stood, went to the cart, grabbed more paper cups, filled them, and started helping as well.

It was all just too amazing for Liz to believe. Those two clearly understood they were being cured by something not approved by doctors, yet they were helping. They must have been really fed up with being held prisoner by the doctors and the army.

A man that Liz had handed a paper cup to on the first row suddenly made a loud sound.

The guy across from him, who was facing the room and watching, shushed him with a perfectly normal hand and arm. Liz didn't know what to do but keep going, dripping water on the sleeping ones, handing the others cups as fast as she could go. It seemed that a lot of people in the room were in on this event, and making sure in one way or another it got done.

Liz finished the row of people she was on, turned to go down the next row, and met the woman again as she finished.

Around them the room was growing louder with talking as more and more people realized they were being cured. A few of the guards started to stir as well, clearly not liking that fact that things right in front of them were changing.

"You two better get out of here," the woman said. "I'll make sure there wasn't anyone you missed."

"Thanks," Liz said. "For the help."

The woman laughed, high and clear and very happy. "No, thank *you*."

Liz smiled and turned and headed for the water cart.

"Leave the cart," Maria said, cutting in front of her and walking quickly toward the stairs. "We just need to find a good place to hole up until things open up around here. I have a hunch we're going to be looked for."

Liz couldn't agree more, but at the moment didn't much care. As the door closed behind them, the sounds were growing as more and more people realized their skin was turning from green back to its normal color.

It was a great sound, that sound of joy.

And it made Liz smile.

Tess was almost back to normal by the time they reached the hospital, and Sheriff Valenti parked his truck in the lot across the street from the main entrance. It seemed that all Tess had needed was a little rest. Now she claimed she'd have no trouble getting them inside.

But Max didn't have any idea at all what to do now that they were at the hospital. Suddenly, with people coming and going, and the army guards at the doors, it didn't seem logical to just go in and start searching the building for Liz and Maria and Isabel.

Yet he had to do something. He needed to know if they had been caught, or if all the patients had been cured before he dared move.

"You have your cell phone?" Max asked, turning to Tess.

She nodded and dug it out of her purse, keeping her body pressed against Max's side as much as she could, as if gaining strength from him.

He took it. Calling Liz's phone wasn't the best idea in the world because its ringing might get her in trouble, but it was the only idea he had at the moment. He had to know what was happening in there. He quickly dialed Liz's cell phone number before he changed his mind.

It rang once, then Liz answered in a very tiny whisper. "Hello."

"Liz?" Max asked, worried about the sound of her voice.

Beside him Tess moved away.

"Max," Liz whispered. "Maria and I are hiding, so I can't talk any louder."

"Where?" Max asked. "Why?"

"In a laundry shoot between the main floor and the basement laundry," she whispered. "We got everyone cured, we think, but a bunch of people saw us do it, so we're letting things calm down before we try moving around."

"Good thinking," Max said. "We got everyone on the base cured as well."

"Great," Liz whispered. "Maria wants to know if you've heard from Michael?"

"No," Max said. "But we haven't been back to the Crashdown yet. Did you find Isabel?"

"She's fine," Liz whispered. "Trapped in a classroom with a bunch of people, but fine."

Suddenly Max knew what had to be done next. If everyone with green skin had been cured in the hospital, and on the army base, then the doctors needed to have an explanation for the press, and for themselves, to believe. And Max, with Tess's help, had just the thing for them.

"Stay put," he said to Liz. "We'll bring you a change of clothes in an hour or so."

"Great," Liz whispered. "Be careful."

"You too," Max said, and hung up. It was a huge relief that Liz and Maria and Isabel were all right.

He handed the phone back to Tess, then turned to the sheriff and repeated all the news that Liz had told him.

"So we have a successful night so far," Valenti said. "Now what?"

"We get Liz and Maria a change of clothes so they don't stand out when they try to leave," Max said. "They were seen curing people with the water."

"Oh," Valenti said.

Max turned to Tess and put his hand on hers. "Are you sure you're feeling all right?"

She nodded, smiling at him. "I'm fine."

"Can you try to plant ideas in a few doctors' minds, sort of like making someone believe we were doctors?"

Tess nodded. "I think so. I could do it like an extended hallucination. It should last for a few hours, or maybe days. Depends on how much the doctors need to believe what you want them to believe, and how close it is to the truth."

"Something easy," Max said, smiling as he held Tess's hand. "And very close. How about we make them think the green skin was caused by a harmless microorganism in the water. Sort of a green tide that came and then went."

"I like it," Valenti said.

"So do I," Tess said, squeezing Max's hand.

"So," Max said to the sheriff, "while Tess and I go in and make some suggestions to a few doctors, can you get our trapped friends a change of clothes?"

"Gladly," Valenti said.

"We'll meet you in the downstairs laundry room in about an hour," Max said. "With luck the army troops should be called off by then."

"We can only hope," Valenti said.

"That we can," Max said, opening the door and helping Tess out. "Well, Doctor," he said to Tess, "are you up for a little visit to a friendly hospital?"

"Ready as I'll ever be, Doctor," she said, laughing.

Together they turned and headed for the front door of the hospital, to clean up the last few details of a very long night.

18

The smell of bacon cooking in the Crashdown was the best thing Max could remember greeting him in a long time. The OPEN sign was out, the sun was up, and a half dozen customers were sitting around the café, reading the paper and drinking orange juice. Michael was in the kitchen talking with the day cook and Alex and Kyle were sitting in a booth, sipping coffee. They both looked tired, dirty, and very beat-up.

"Success?" Max asked Alex. Liz, Tess, Maria, Isabel, and the sheriff followed Max through the door.

"Success," Alex said, smiling, "but at a price."

Max didn't like the sound of that, but with normal customers in the restaurant and the day waitress two booths over helping a nice couple, he wasn't going to press.

Michael came out of the kitchen, also looking beat-up and tired. He reached into his pocket and tossed the sheriff a set of keys. "Thanks."

"Don't mention it," the sheriff said, smiling.

"Oh, trust me, I won't if you won't," Michael said. He

looked at Max, shook his head, and went back into the kitchen.

Now Max was really worried. But at least they were all here, and the treated water was in the ground.

"Ready to go home, son?" Valenti asked Kyle.

"I'm ready to go home and stay home," Kyle said, slowly easing himself out of the booth and limping toward the door. The sheriff held the door open for his son, a puzzled expression on his face.

Max just shrugged and the sheriff quickly moved to open the truck door for Kyle.

"What *happened* to you guys?" Maria asked.

"You don't want to know," Alex said, "and we don't want to tell you at the moment."

"Oh," Liz said, "that bad, huh?" She slipped in beside Alex.

"Yes," Alex said, trying to sip his coffee with shaking hands.

Maria sat in the booth across from him.

Tess took a spot at the counter while Isabel slid into the booth next to Maria.

Max decided to stand so he could see everyone. At the moment he wanted everyone's story, but knew that with regular customers listening, he was going to have to wait.

"I'm assuming," Alex said, looking around, "from your smiling faces, that the night was a success."

"Completely," Max said. "The doctors discovered the green skin was caused by a harmless microorganism. The paper is calling it 'the Green Tide' and making fun of it."

Tess winked at him and he winked back. It felt good to work so closely with Tess. He wasn't sure why, and he wasn't sure he wanted to push it farther than that. The future would tell on that score.

"It wasn't much fun being locked up in a classroom all night, though," Isabel said. "Boring beyond belief. And I don't think Rob's ever going to want to date me again."

"After he turned green on the first one, why would he?" Alex asked.

"Must not have been too rough a night," Maria said. "Your sense of humor is coming back."

"I just rode ten miles in the back of a horse trailer," Alex said. "I have no sense of humor."

"Or smell," Maria said.

Isabel and Tess laughed.

Max couldn't help but grin himself. He was feeling very good that they had escaped this problem, mostly intact. It could have been a lot worse.

But Alex had yet to see the humor in the morning. Or the previous day's events.

His face turned slowly red under the dirt. "Yesterday afternoon my entire body was green." His voice carried through the entire restaurant. "Every inch of my skin was that color. I don't find anything funny about *that*."

"Sorry," Maria said, trying to calm Alex and get him to lower his voice.

"Nothing to be sorry about," Alex said. "You know what it felt like. But just tell me what I would have done if the color would have stayed?"

Maria and Isabel both shrugged.

"Come on," Alex said. "You have all the answers. How would I have managed for the rest of my life if the green skin had become permanent?"

Max glanced around the café. Sitting in the back booth was a black couple, both listening and drinking coffee. Two stools down from Tess was a Native American, also clearly listening. And at the cash register waiting for someone to take her money was a woman with bright red hair.

None of them offered an answer to Alex's question, although Max was sure each of them had one.